T0103809

Pursuit of Freedom

Pursuit of Freedom

Laxmi Parasuram

ISBN:	Softcover	978-1-4828-7491-4
	eBook	978-1-4828-7490-7

Print information available on the last page.

To order additional copies of this book, contact
Partridge India
000 800 10062 62
orders.india@partridgepublishing.com

www.partridgepublishing.com/india

CONTENTS

PREFACE

PURSUIT OF FREEDOM depicts the story of a journey in search of FREEDOM in all its ramifications from the perspective of an Indian girl. This journey is undertaken by Maya, a girl born in a remote village in Kerala, when people had heard only about political freedom from colonial rule. Maya's journey for freedom reaches out for more complex perspectives since it starts from pre-independent India and concludes in the modern age of rapid social changes including human rights, democracy and globalization.

Maya's initial struggle for freedom is against her own family, their feudal high caste rules and norms as well as patriarchal authority. As she rebels and leaves her family she is exposed to different ways of life amidst different people at different periods. Her escape from home was in search of education which she was denied, and from an arranged marriage which she refused. The impact of Gandhi and Freedom movement, the evils of caste rivalries as well as feudal and communist ideas filter through her mind in her determined rebellion against all forms of established ideas.

Maya apart from being an individual also becomes a symbol for her country that has been going through varied experiences, changes and influences during these years. Her journey undertaken to challenge rigid traditionalism and colonialism leads to a sense of egalitarianism, globalization and an understanding of true freedom. While in America, the land of Freedom and Democracy, an exposure to diversity and multiculturalism turn into agonizing factors to create a sense of cultural disorientation. Her American Dream of Freedom and Equality can no longer be accepted in simple faith, and the ideal of a Melting Pot of differences cannot be validated as reality

The story is told through other people's perspective, particularly in the beginning, since the social framework that Maya rebels against has to be presented through different participants. Ammalu and Velayudhan who work for the family give their impressions as onlookers, and Sekhar, the center of patriarchal power, dramatizes Maya's story until her escape from home bringing significant details. Later sections are more focused on Maya herself and her psychological and spiritual struggles. The turmoils within her mind between India and America, faith and doubt, reality and illusion are projected through her varied experiences. Sister Sacramenta in the second section acts as a caring mother and a beacon of light to Maya's confused mind. The use of flashbacks in the American sections emphasize the cultural contrasts in Maya's experiences.

The American Dream that valorizes the idea that one can totally unburden oneself from the past and lead a life free from all social pressures, influences and dependencies is examined in the book through personal experiences. It is not the achievement of freedom, but a personal sense of the widening gyres of freedom that the book brings to the readers.

Since the first section of the book is located in Kerala in South India a few ethnic words from the local language, Malayalam, are used and a glossary is attached to give English equivalents.

Laxmi Parasuram
Prof.of English and
American Literature (Retd.)

An M.A. from Bombay University and a Ph.D. from the University of Kentucky, Dr Laxmi Parasuram's experience of the academic world spans 25 years as a Professor of English in India. She is the recipient of both British and American awards, including the Visit award from the British Council and Fulbright post-doctoral Fellowships from the U.S. She is the past President of the Indian Association for American Studies and has contributed several papers on American Literature studies in India. She has also edited a volume entitled American Literature and Culture and written a critical book on Virginia Woolf called Virginia Woolf: the Emerging Reality. As an Inner Wheel member of the Rotary Club of South West Calcutta, she has written its history. She is also a member of the Rotary Club of Calcutta South City Towers. Her first novel published in 2003 is *Entrapped in Academia.* An active member of Soroptimist International, she has served in local and national committees of this global association for professional women.

TO AMERICA WITH LOVE

"So free we seem, so fettered fast we are"

Robert Browning

"We, and all others who believe as deeply as we do, would rather die on our feet than live on our knees."

Franklin D Roosevelt

Professor Robert Hamburger teaches Creative Writing and American Literature at New Jersey City University. He has twice served as a Senior Fulbright Lecturer in India. His six books cover a variety of genres: oral history, personal journalism, biography, travel memoir, and fiction. His most recent works are A Passage Through India {Spuyten Duyvil Press, 1998) and Shiraz (XOXOX Press, 2006)

FOREWORD

The year is 1940 and colonial India is in the throes of transformation. Inspired by heroic leaders and blazing rhetoric, the freedom movement has taken root throughout the land. But what does this mean for twelve year old Maya, the spirited Kerala girl whose life we follow in *Pursuit of Freedom?* Change is in the air -there is talk of Gandhi and of throwing off the British yoke - yet Maya remains ensnared in age-old forms of bondage that predate the British presence and will extend well into decades of Indian nationhood. A mere child, Maya is expected to passively accept the arranged marriage her parents have selected for her; she is expected to accept a future built upon the mysterious (to a prepubescent child) duties of sexual submission, childbearing, and housekeeping; she is expected to understand that for girls there is no point in hoping for more than a rudimentary education; and she is expected to submit to the stern wisdom of the Bhagawat Gita that "joy and sorrow had to be accepted in the same spirit."

These are the overwhelming obstacles that young Maya faces. Yet a fierce spirit of independence, or rather, of self-preservation, compels her to rebel. Against the massed forces of tradition, religion, and parental authority Maya is thrown back upon what the Quakers call her "inner light" to guide her. Is she strong enough to forge a life of her own choosing? And at what cost? These are central questions that drive Laxmi Parsuram's compelling narrative: at once a poignant study of an individual life, as well as a challenging examination of the obstacles to women's freedom that remain embedded in Indian culture to this very day. Here is young Maya reflecting on her situation after she has rebuffed her parents' first attempt at marrying her:

> "So that guy who stared at me and glued his eyes to my face will not marry me! Should I rejoice at this news or shall I join my mother and Ammalu and be sorry for myself No! I do not want to get married and if they start with another proposal I will not agree. But my father! He will stop me from going to school just to teach me a lesson as he says. Then what will happen to all my plans to study and earn my own living? "Why do you want to earn money?" they ask me, "your father has more than enough. He will hand you over to a husband who can keep you in style and give you all you need. Study and earn money! Is that what you want? Do you want to look for a job as a clerk or nurse and do some dirty work all day? You don't know what men outside can do to you. Better submit to what your own family asks you to do..." (43)

Given these formidable obstacles, Maya's journey to liberation is lonely and psychologically painful, but her resolve is strengthened by a handful of teachers and allies she encounters. When she trades her gold bangles for the opportunity to study Hindi, her teacher, Vasudevan Nair, explains that enlightened members of his caste believe in full equality for women, including property rights and civil rights. In fact, it is their custom for the man to marry into his wife's family. "Women marry according to their wish... Marriage is not compulsory," (74) he tells her. Here is a vision of freedom that addresses Maya's innermost promptings. When Maya questions him about the power of religion, he replies, "I am not superstitious. I don't see God in a stone." (74) However, Maya's tutelage is brought to an abrupt end when she joins her teacher at a day-long gathering of Hindi scholars and students. Her father gets wind of her transgression and puts an abrupt end to her education.

With her father blocking her path to enlightenment, Maya falls into a deep depression. If she cannot live by her own aptitudes and desires and dreams, what is there to live for? She begs her father to send her to a convent school, a request that outrages him and leads to a brutal beating. With all hope gone, she seizes a kitchen knife and implores her father to relieve her of her suffering: "You brought me into this world unasked for, and you have fed me on shame and anguish all my life. Take away my life now since I don't care to have it any longer." (94) Yet it is this very moment of resignation that liberates her. Sekhar, her father, sees that custom and paternal authority have no power to break his daughter's will. "Our whole world is turning topsy-turvy," he discovers, "and this girl, the wildest of my own seeds, challenges me and threatens to make me feel like a woman ..." (95) Here, at this crucial juncture, "the hand of authority, the hold of custom, melted away into the thin air of uncertainty ..." (96) and he consents to her convent school education.

Convent school, with its separation from Maya's contentious home, its freedom from caste, and its husbandless woman teachers, offers a measure of relief - but it is not the oasis she dreamed of. The school welcomes non-Catholic students, yet it still imposes a strict examination of conscience on the young girls. The school's relentless moralizing leads to inevitable disciplinary problems. A careless girl deposits a bloody menstrual rag in the toilet and is so upset with her supposed sin that she vows to go home and get married. In her moral instruction class, Maya is informed that only God can bring real happiness. When Maya pragmatically proposes that many people are quite happy without God, that they are content "eating, drinking, playing and earning money" (112) she is instantly marked as a troublemaker. Maya is also troubled by occasional accounts of love and physical desire. After her harrowing resistance to child marriage, there is no place in her thoughts or actions for gestures of affection. She recoils at her friend, Theresa's, physical overtures and is utterly baffled by her declarations of love. Not surprisingly, the convent sisters' promise of God's love is equally unattractive. "I want to be free, Sister," Maya declares. "I want to be able to earn my own living, live in a real world without being always told what I should do and how I should always be grateful and obedient." (135) As her sojourn at convent school draws to a close, Maya reflects "It was not like this before. I had an excess of self-confidence but now it is as though I am being dragged through a process of uncertainty and helplessness. Would you say that I have only to pray and keep quiet?" (149)

Now, Maya's journey brings her to an American university where she pursues her studies in the socially permissive environment of "the land of the free." With half the planet separating her from the confining strictures of India, it would seem that at last Maya is free to be herself and follow her own. But nothing is simple. Maya is utterly unprepared for the casual sexual mores of Greenwich Village, the warnings about V.D., or an offhanded classroom lecture on Hemingway in which her teacher expounds on "that great machismo of a writer [who] was good at hunting and at f...ing" (161) Is this the freedom she fought for at such great cost? Maya retreats into literature. "Books had now become more real to me than my own life that had shrunken to the size of the crumpled face of a clock" (171). Her Indian classmate, Pankaj, the child of a conservative Brahmin family, falls in love with an American boy; her American classmate, Judy, falls in love with an Indian boy - and Maya is equally confounded by both these relationships. "In America, almost everyone spoke of love and frequently fell into it," she reflects. But little has changed since her convent days. In one of the novel's most memorable passages, Maya expresses her dread of the sexual obligations she associates with love.

> I could not even say the word LOVE... it stuck in my throat and pulled down my tongue ... it made me look pink and awkward ... it had something to do with the flesh I hated and felt apologetic about, it resembled the long red dripping tongue of cows licking the gummy, hairy back of new-born calves, the roguish eyes of bulls turning to hazy red as they wagged their stiff tails trying to caress and mount the backs of she-animals with throaty, husky moos and hoarse breathings (l 85)

Not surprisingly, Maya feels revolted by her classmates' glib responses to Whitman's bold emphasis on the link between bodily and spiritual freedom. "When I read poems I get carried away by the ring and movement of words... their pitch and evocative quality ... the truth of their claims and splendid associations ... but here in America to be an academic is to analyze, rip apart and generate sexual explanations. I must confess that I am unfit for such operations ... am I being forced to change to remake myself?" (203) Life in America appears to offer free living and freedom of expression, but Maya sniffs the poisonous fumes of conformity and digs in her heels. And how truly open-minded is America? When Maya nervously agrees to join a Pakistani boy at an offcampus bar, her adventure ends when a bunch of men taunt them as "blackies trying to ape the west" and beat up her escort.

America is tainted for Maya. She peers through the veil of America's self-congratulatory image to gaze upon its unsavoury, unspoken reality. As she puts it, "the American Experiment remains the greatest human effort to liberate humanity from the intrusions of the truth of [the] human condition."

(227) The outbreak of the Bangladesh War draws Maya back to India. Her parents are aging, her beloved servant is dead, her siblings have slipped into jobs and marriage, and the tempo of village life has forever changed. "I had a hazy feeling that I had not left America," she muses. "Our old country was remaking itself along modem lines ... when the old giant heaves itself out of its long slumber it will surely wear an American overcoat..." (233). So for all her struggles, after years of tenaciously defending her innermost being, Maya remains embattled. Her situation is reminiscent of those lines in Matthew Arnold's great poem, "Stanzas From the Grand Chartreuse," where the speaker positions himself:

> Wandering between two worlds, one dead,
> The other powerless to be born,
> With nowhere yet to rest my head ...

Maya's struggle continues. But if there is no "happy ending" to her embattled life, there is the precious certainty that she has defended her integrity against overwhelming forces. To call Laxmi Parasuram's heartfelt narrative an important feminist text would be merely stating the obvious. One can surely view Maya's story as an illuminating examination of the fissures that opened in Indian life at the time of Independence - and their immense personal consequences. But above all, Pursuit of Freedom, is more than a "women's novel" or an "Indian novel." It is a richly imagined and deeply felt testimony to the timeless human impulse that informs all our lives: to find some measure of freedom from the shaping powers of country, custom, religion, and family.

Dr. Robert Hamburger
Professor of English:
New Jersey City University

HOME

"Life is not that which one lived, but that which one remembers and how one remembers to tell it."

Gabriel Garcia Marquez

I

MAYA 1940

"They are coming to see the girl today," said Ammalu, 'they' meaning two women from that far-off town, Tiruvananthapuram, (the capital of old Travancore state) and 'the girl' meaning me. "They will be accompanied by two or three men from the family and the young man who is looking for a girl to marry," she added.

This group of five whose arrival was being proclaimed by Ammalu seemed to be like headhunters (weren't they in fact woman-hunters!) and the girl they were planning to hunt happened to be ME! As soon as I had heard Ammalu, I crawled noiselessly under the cot in the vast store room in our sprawling house.

"Maya! Maya!" I could now hear my mother's faint cries and these were soon taken up by others in the family. Was it Ammalu again or was it Kunji now adding her shrill voice to my mother's? "Mayakutty! Mayakutty!" shouted Kunji, our old maid servant, a haggard old woman, in fact, but who still had a piercing voice. Ammalu, of course, was much younger, our cook and virtual mother, and the chorus of their calls for me came to me in waves over the pickle jars behind which I crouched. "Where are you? Come and dress up, girl ... they are coming to see the girl!"

I was getting somewhat choked up under that cot. Sacks full of rice and lentils were stacked up behind me and I had folded and thrust my heavy bottom in between two bags of lentils. The tall jar of pickles in front kept me fairly well hidden. I kept mum and controlled my breath.

"Mayakutty, where are you?" I could now hear Velu coming nearer. He said something to my mother and started moving the pickle jars. Before he reached out for my shrinking body parts, I jumped out and lay exposed on the floor.

"She needs to be thrashed" someone shouted. "Don't, don't," my mother was pleading.

"Let her not start crying now ... on this auspicious day. I shall get her ready before they come."

So I was dragged to the bathroom and Kunji poured mugfuls of hot and cold water upon me and started scrubbing with a fibrous sponge (I knew where it came from ... from that tree at the back of our house I used to climb... they were dried pods that came very handy to scrub oneself...) Wrapped in a long towel I was all ready to be made up as a possible bride... my hair pulled left and right and dabbed with coconut oil... kajal applied around my eyes to make them doe-like, kumkum on my forehead and yards and yards of silk around my body. I wiggled and writhed, but was soon turned into a doll willy-nilly.

II

MAYA

They were watching me closely as I entered the front room with my head bent. I could see the red tiles under my feet with the corner of my eyes. Someone pushed me down to take a seat on the floor.

Conversation went on around me and I could hear that it was all about me.

"She is now in Class 5," my uncle was saying, "She is always at the top of her class".

"Has she learnt some music? Some cooking?"

"I don't think she has any interest in music ... Well, as a family we are not much into music and that sort of thing ..."

"What do you like to do, girl, after your marriage?"

I realized that the question was addressed to me, a bit late of course since I was not expecting it.

I raised my eyes to look at the scene around me. A young man sitting quietly in the middle of it all was about to devour me with his eyes.

"I would like to study," I said.

If there was any consternation at my answer I was not aware of it, I only knew that someone helped me rise from my sitting position and I was marched off to the next room.

When the farewells had been said and the visitors seen off, my mother and father conferred together on the possible outcome of this visit." Do you think they would agree to this alliance after having seen Maya? Doesn't she look very pretty and grown-up?"

"What is there to see so much?" My father retorted rather loudly. "All that remains is to take her clothes off and then see... Ha ... ha ... ha ..."(a loud guffaw)

III

AMMALU

I just heard Sekhar laughing in that unholy way of his ... What did he say so loudly for all to hear? Didn't he say something about taking the clothes off the girl to see her properly? Stripping her naked ... was that it...? Is that all a man sees in a girl?

My own life tells me something different. My husband ... God bless him... died 30 years ago when I was only fourteen. Doesn't it tell you how old I am now ... does it tell you all that I have gone through as a widow for these many years?

"Akka! Akka!"

"Oh, that is Saras calling me as she always does. She is the mother and wife in this house, married to Sekhar from the age of thirteen to give birth to at least a dozen children (God bless her! She lost six of them still born and had one or two miscarriages in addition!). She is worried about her eldest girl, Maya, now, since that girl is always is found at the wrong place at the wrong time... wanting to be more like a boy than a girl and talking as if she is going to do so many things ... today she was found hiding under the cot in the store room when people from a decent family came to negotiate her marriage ..."

"AKKA! AKKA!"

"I am coming! I am coming, Saras!"

"Akka, where are you? Do you hear me? Always day- dreaming, are you?"

"No! Saras, I am not daydreaming ... What is there to dream for me?"

"Okay, Okay ... The evening meal will be served at 8 p.m. today and I hope you will tell Kunji to get the children ready. We will have sambhar and tapioca fry tonight along with those left-over sweets made for the family who came to see Maya."

"I will see to that... Don't you worry, Saras."

Daydreaming ... that is what she always blames me for... Do I have any dreams left now... only the tears from my past are left with me... and my hopes for a better deal in my next birth when my Lord and master who left me so suddenly after only two years of marriage will seek me out again.

No! No! It can never be as Sekhar says ... Do men look for women only for what is under their clothes ...? Then how about me who did not even once enjoy the thrill of being sought there... Married at twelve to an ailing man of 50... I nursed and prayed for him all through those two years I lived with him and then he left me alone to work for others...

The children have started coming in. They look freshly scrubbed and washed, their limbs kick about like rubber balls, their faces bright and smiling like Lord Krishna's as he played in Gokul ... Let me get busy now ...

IV

Maya

This is the large room in the middle of my house where my brothers, sisters and cousins are flocking for their evening meal... they scream and shout and laugh ... they vibrate and scintillate the whole room with their overflowing energy ... the quick movements of their limbs, their roving eyes and the turns and twists of their faces beckon me to join them as a child although they have now declared me marriageable ... old enough to leave this house and my people and live with strangers. In the middle of the room sits our large kerosene lamp and we find our seats on the floor around the lamp. Our silver plates gleam in the half shadows cast by the lamp.

Those twisted branches of our large mango tree outside act as a pall on the tiled roof of our dining room, and patches of darkness roam around us when the thick foliage on those branches sway to the winds outside. Our windows are barred to keep the insects off and we cannot hear even the bird cries other than those occasional hoots of an owl sitting on one of those dark branches. Ramunna had quietly taken me out one night in the dark and pointed to the sour face of that owl ready to hoot.

All's still now until pots of rice, dal, curries, and papadams are brought by Ammalu Athai, Meenu and others. Balu grabs a whole papadam and it breaks into pieces ... he starts to howl.

"Keep quiet, Balu!" That was Ammalu trying to take charge of the situation and trying to stop Balu from howling.

"I want another whole one," insists Balu.

"How will you eat if it is not broken?" argues Pankaj. "I want to hold it," says Balu.

"Here take it," says Ammalu.

Our poor Ammalu Athai! She is always trying to bring peace among us. She is our mediator. We go to her crying and come back strangely consoled.

They say that her husband died when she was only fourteen! Oh! How old she must have been when she married? Must be 11 or 12, since she lived with him only for 2 or 3 years. Well, that is my age now and they are trying to get me married. But, no, I will not agree to that.

My plate is full... there is a mound of rice on it slapped with thick gravy and floating vegetables. I can hear the sounds of gulping and chewing. Someone shouts for water, he must have bitten a chilli. I bend and take my food from the plate and carry it to the mouth almost with a sleight of hand.

We can now hear a rustle from the leaves of trees outside. Some stirrings and crackling sounds are heard and there is a hue and cry among the children who get up and run to the window. "Who's that? Who's that?" they whisper. "There is something moving," someone says under his breath. Balu keeps his mouth open and listens. They all crowd under the hanging kerosene lamp and it dangles to and fro, its shadows melting into one another to form a tilting giant form. They are all frightened and look to their elders for solace. The sound of a branch being broken, a fresh rustle of leaves and a faint guffaw from outside leave them almost shitting in their pants. Then, I, Maya, whom everyone calls a daredevil, gather myself and move towards the window to pose a bold question... "Who? Who are you?" A long silence follows during which even the fall of a leaf could be heard. And then, the long sought-for answer comes in a gruff, sonorous voice, "Your mother's husband!" Ha! Ha! It was after all the old man prowling under the mango trees and frightening his own children! Then, a rising gust of amusement checked cautiously with incredulity follows and strangely hushed, the poor herd go back timidly to their seats to finish the cold repast.

After finishing our meal, when the children began to play and talk to each other, Meenu, our regular help in the kitchen, came out and sat down with me. She was my classmate in school when both of us were in the primary, but she had since been taken out of the school to assist in our kitchen. She was particularly fond of narrating ghost stories she had heard from her mother and drawing me closer to her in rapt attention.

"You know what happened last Sunday", she started. "Appu Sar and Velu had to go to the Thevara, our next village, at night to call a midwife. They had to walk on a road next to the 'smasan' (burning ghat) carrying a little smoke-bound, flickering wicker lamp dangling from Velu's hand. Dark moving shadows spread around them like the mighty arms of monsters eager to grab them and suddenly they saw a wave of blackness advancing towards them beyond the ken of their little light. They heard the clutter of running hoofs not far from the fields where the cows had strayed in daytime, and at a distance they could see a tiny light from a pyre where a body, numb and partly burnt perhaps, had been mounted beneath a pile of raw wood. Gleams from a ray of white light, incandescent and ethereal, were moving around the pyre as if some fretful visitation from the other world were searching for fresh habitations there. Appu Sar and Velu took to their heels as soon as they saw this white light and started mumbling those Sanskrit mantras they had learnt by rote from the village Brahmin. And you know what happened? As soon as they started chanting Gayatri, that white light trembled and melted and had disappeared when they looked back. So, Maya, this is the story people are now talking about in the village." Meenu concluded her exciting narration.

"But Meenu, today my father tried to frighten us and some of us were scared as if it was a ghost prowling under the mango tree. Similarly, it might just have been one of the mourners at the pyre with a little light that went out in the breeze that scared Ayya Sar and Velu."

"No! No! we have to believe that ghosts are real.. They are the forces of evil."

"Maybe we should all learn Gayatri, then we can scare those evil forces!"

"No, Maya, no Gayatri for women! They won't even let us hear it. We have to depend on men for our protection."

I shuddered at the thought of my own life-long dependent status on men needing their protection. But Meenu did not seem to care and she went on to other stories recounting several lurking fears that unsettled the minds of villagers. She told Maya in confidential whispers how that carpenter Sankaran who so quietly chiselled wood and built benches during the day was stark drunk in the evening and roamed the streets with his hammer and chisel abusing everyone.

"Oh!" I exclaimed. "I know Sankaran. He came to our house the other day after the sun had set and the gates were fully closed, and he shouted, 'Valya

Sarni! Valya Sarni!' My father went up to him with his big stick and asked him, 'how did you come in here when the gates are closed?' And you know what he said... "I came like a fox, Valya Sarni! I came rolling under the gate." Then he made a loud guffaw provoking all of us to laugh. Then you know what ... My father raised his stick and told him, 'you roll back now under that gate or I am going to beat you black and blue.' And the poor chap looked up frightened and went quietly to the gate and rolled back outside. My father then turned to me angrily and said, 'what are you here for? Go inside. That fellow is drunk.'"

"But, Maya," Pankaj said, "You shouldn't be standing there and watching such people. Your father is right. You don't know what drunks like him can do."

"What can they do?"

"Well, they can even try to rape you if they feel like it."

"What is rape? Do you mean that he will try to beat me? Whenever I talk to him he is very nice ... I mean when he is not drunk."

"Maya, you don't know anything. You have to be careful with men. They can do many things to you." Then she giggled in that quiet way of hers and started talking in low whispers.

"You should go to Mala's house and see what happened to her," she muttered, "All because of a man she got close to. She was secretly meeting him and did all she was asked to do just to please him. And then, she had something growing in her tummy and her people are torturing her."

"What did she do to make that thing grow in her tummy?" "Maya, you are indeed stupid... Don't you know what happens when you go close to a man? You have to get married before you go so close and do that thing. I can tell you this only in your ear." Meenu again giggled and tried to pinch me between my thighs.

"Go away, Meenu. Now I see Ramunna coming and I want to talk to him."

Ramunna had come in quietly and was now sitting in our midst. He was our star and inspiration, a leader to whom we looked up to as a hero. He had a bicycle of his own and he went to places riding on it.

Annante cycline bell illa, brake illa,

Mudguard illa chanted the children for him to hear. That song had always put Ramunna in a good mood and he was all smiles as he sat near them.

Bell illa, brake illa, seat illa, tube illa, chain illa, pedal illa ... continued the song in a chorus... This song was made up by Ramunna himself when his cycle had broken down after a fall on the rough roads of the village, and when he was pleading for a new cycle.(The song was about the breakdown of the different parts of his cycle which were to be replaced

"Can you please give me a ride on the back of your bike?" asked Balu.

"Can you teach me how to ride?" I asked as I always did and he turned round saying, "You are a girl... a girl... girls don't ride bikes."

"Why is the sky blue, Ramunna?" That was Pankaj who always stared at the sky as in a trance.

"Guagua, Guagua, Guagua," said Ramunna in his own familiar style.(He always said this when he did not know the answer)

"Can you tell me which came first, the egg or the chicken?" that was Pankaj again.

"GUAGUA, GUAGUA, GUAGUA!" they all repeated laughing along with Ramunna

"Have you caught a squirrel today?" asked Hari who was usually quiet. He liked to go and look at the squirrels caught by Ramunna by keeping a piece of banana inside a cage and setting a trap.

"No! No!" replied he, "that squirrel has slipped away. You will see what I will do tomorrow".

"Shall we call that squirrel Shivaji?" I asked. I had just remembered my history lesson giving the story of Shivaji slipping away from the prison of Aurangazebe.

"I will give you a tongue twister," said Ramunna. "Let me see who can say it fastest... Just go on saying, 'she sells seashells on the sea shore' faster and faster ... who can say it fastest of all?"

Then they all started saying it trying to be faster and faster until the words twisted and slipped off their tongues.

V

AMMALU

Just to see and hear these children feels like sunshine on my chill hands and numb back. My womb never opened out to bring forth a child nor did I suckle one and hear the tender lisps of my own flesh and blood. But these children make me tremble with joy like mine own... what else do I have in this life?

He left me alone and passed away. How I ran to fetch the doctor in the middle of that night when he started coughing and coughing without a break, (not that he did not cough at other times ... even as he sat in our marriage panda! tying a knot on my mangal sutra with all those nadaswarams and drums going on all around, I had heard him go into a fit of coughing ... his sister then had tried to sooth his throat with a gulp of some medicine or was it only water?), but on that last night his cough was incessant and feeble... he had spat so much blood and he could barely signal to me to call the doctor. I was to bring him luck, he had often said ... I was to prolong his life for many years with the strength and power of my mangal sutra (made with four sovereigns of pure 22ct. gold!) Oh! What gifts I had carried to those deities sitting in temples with shapely eyes, short limbs and often pouched bellies ... how often had I cruised around those stone walls of the temples with closed eyes and a mind that enthroned a sick and feeble figure, my Lord and master, for life, who came to marry me and take me to his own house. I was to be the guardian of his good luck, a loving nurse to his tubercular body and a virtual mother to his three children from his first marriage ... I never asked him about his first wife... only the children told me that their mother was this and that... but I loved them as my own and looked after them for two whole years.

And then that long and tragic night... I had run around his bed giving him syrups and medicines, fomenting his chest and shedding tears and praying, then those never ending bouts of coughing that brought out clots of blood and phlegm. I ran to the doctor's house with a lump in my throat and a pair of shivering limbs that knocked against each other ... I brought the doctor home only to find my beloved husband rolling on the bed with a violent spasm of pain, covered all over with sweat and his own bloody spit. The doctor, with a gesture of throwing up his hands, opened his black bag, took out a syringe and wanted to disinfect it. *Oh! How slow these doctors are!* I ran to the kitchen to get a pot of hot water ... the syringe was cleaned and the shot given. Then a peace seemed to descend on his fretful breathings, the ascending lumps of cough that had been seen to roll up his chest now seemed to slacken, relax and finally settle down. But he never opened his eyes again ... and left me all alone to fend for myself thus.

"Athai! Athai! Where are you?"

That's Balu calling me. He will not leave me alone even for a minute. He wants me to hitch up his trousers, wipe his nose and mediate in his fights with Hari. Is he not indeed a cherub from the other world bringing me tidings of joy!

"Yes, Balu, what do you want?"

"Athai, Just look at Hari ... he is pushing me away from Ramunna. I want to sit close to him and hear the story. And can you give me a banana, please. I have finished my dinner leaving nothing on the plate."

"Okay, Balu. Be quiet."

Yes, this is Ramu's evening treat for them. He keeps them glued to his stories. He has a knack with children that is amazing. And his stories... he changes and adds to them every time he gets a chance. Truth or hearsay, Ramu's stories draw a rapt audience!

VI

MAYA

The light from that dusky kerosene lamp falls directly on Ramunna's face as he tries to sit facing all of us. His face is brown and his eyebrows are black and arched somewhat like those of mythical figures I have seen in pictures. His broad forehead, moving up and down quickly as he reaches his narrative pitch fascinates me and I often fail to look at his mouth that is lit with flashes from his shining teeth. I have heard his stories several times, but every time they seem different.

"Tell me who Ram was," he begins.

"He was our great grandfather, wasn't he?" they clamour together. "You are named after him, aren't you?"

"He was the man who planted this mango tree," said Pankaj "But let me tell you what he was in the beginning," Ramunna started his story. "Ram was only a poor little boy who did not even have enough to eat and he roamed around the streets in torn clothes. His own mother died when he was two years old and he had a step mother."

"And then?"

"He wanted to make his way through the world and he did not want to stay at home washing clothes and cleaning utensils for his step mother. So one day he climbed on to a bullock cart and hid himself under the clothes piled on it."

"Oh! I know what HE DID NEXT ... when the night came, did he not raise his head and look around? He then tried to get down ..."

"No, he got down only much later. In fact only when the cart passed by our village several miles from where he started. He then went up to the driver of the cart and asked him why he was carrying piles of loincloths in the cart. When the driver said they were for sale, Ram offered to go round the village and sell them. The driver agreed to give him a small commission and so started Ram's first business. He then got richer and richer and made a small house for himself. He also found himself a wife to look after the house and started another business to make much more money."

"What did he do to get more money?"

"He got more money by giving money to those who needed it... I mean, he lent money to those who were short of money and they gave him their land and gold for him to keep until they returned his money. But most of them could not return the money and so Ram could have all the land and gold in his village. He became the richest man in our village and they started calling him 'Valya Sarni' -the Big Master. So you know how our family came and how we became the landlords of this place."

"Will you also become the richest man, Ramunna?"

"Maybe. But I want to become an officer in the government. I want to go to college first."

"Can we all go to college?"

"No, I don't think the girls can. They will have to get married."

VII

Ammalu

Yes ... that is the story that is told again and again in this house. It is the story of old Ram, the first head of this family, they tell each other instead of the story of Ramayana. This house was first built by old Ram years ago when he came to this village as a rising star. His son rebuilt it with several more rooms to accommodate the growing family. And what stories people have built around old Ram, that first progenitor, 'Valya Sarni' as he is called! He came to this village with those loincloths and sold them to everyone - did anyone wear anything at all before he came, I wonder! Maybe they were all going stark naked for all I know. They all fell for those loincloths from across Tamil Nadu and made him rich. He ruled over them with his iron will and took possession of all the land and gold. He became the Grand Master (Valya Sarni) and everyone in the village -young, old, male and female - were like slaves to him, hovering around like flies for a mouthful. And he did marry our village girl, the daughter of a farmer whom he had turned a pauper... but he paid the father an ample sum for the hand of his daughter. I know this for sure, since Mangalam - the girl he married - was none other than my own grandmother's cousin. Oh! She was really beautiful as a picture, lime-coloured with a demure face and doe-like eyes. No wonder 'Valya Sarni' almost fell in love with her (was 'love' ever in his vocabulary, some people wonder!). He was as black as the devil himself... it was Mangalam who implanted the white strain in the black blood of this family. She lay by his side for eight years (until she died of anaemia and childbearing) and produced four sons and a daughter ...

"Amalu ... Amalu ... where are you? Are you daydreaming again?"

That must be Saras again to call me to my chores ... now that the children have eaten, all the elders will gather for their evening meals... I must go ...

A row of banana leaves laid in a straight line, with only the last one slightly turned to face the others. The grand dame of the family, Sekhar's mother, generally known as Mannipatty sat against the last banana leaf to face the others who were seated in a row. Sekahar always came first, loud and booming, shouting something or other to the children who wandered around after their meal. Then came the others, Venkatesh, Subramaniam and Narayanan who are Sekhar's younger brothers. They all live together in the vast family mansion, but meet each other only during the evening meals. Ram, the eldest of Sekhar's children sat next to Mannipatti who beamed at him and exchanged whispers. When they all had sat down on the floor covered with square shaped mats set against the banana leaves, we started going around serving them portions from different items.

The male members were the first to start with a propitiation to the deities with water sprinkled around their leaves... even the water from any of the wells could turn to Ganga water when a few mantras were chanted to it. Then they bent down to begin their meals using their bare hands.

Sekhar was the first to speak. He cleared his throat and addressed his mother.

"Manni," he said, "That Shuppan's family who came here for an alliance with ours has backed out."

"Do you mean the ones who came for Maya?" asked Narayanan, the youngest of the brothers.

Manni who sat with some difficulty on the floor kept trying to swallow before she joined the conversation. She could not bend one of her legs stricken with arthritis and she let it remain spread eagled on the floor while she tried to keep the other in its place with a little pressure from her left hand.

"Yes, they sent a message today through Manickam. They say that their son Nanu would wait for two more years before he made his decision on marriage."

"Then why did they come here? Does it mean that they do not approve of the girl?"

"Well, who knows! With all these tantrums our girl put up it is like trying to sell a lame cow ... Ha! Ha! But our family ... Valya Sami's family will always win at the end. If Shuppan wants to hide behind excuses let him ... Some other better party will turn up for Maya. But I may have to teach that girl how to behave."

Venkatesh now raised his head from looking at his banana leaf As he chewed up a drumstick in the sambhar more thoroughly, he turned to his elder brother.

"Do you know that Maya shows her rebellious ways even at school? Nanu Sar was telling me that she keeps asking awkward questions in the class and distracting everyone. Not that she is not the best in her class... she keeps scoring top ranking marks ... but she asks unnecessary questions."

"Yes, that is another thing I have to attend to ... What do all these studies and schools do for a girl? As long as she has learnt how to sign her name and add two and two she may well be taken out of school. Some of those teachers can turn her head and she may get all the wrong notions."

The meal was over after a last course of rice and buttermilk. While the others got up nimbly from their seats, the old woman struggled to rise to her feet. I quickly came to her side to help and lead her to the washroom.

So that's it... Maya need not be pushed into a marriage just now since the party does not want a marriage now. But a girl is a girl... she has to be married sometime ... Sekhar would have given her a hefty dowry and celebrate the marriage in great style. But she missed her chance this time... let her be careful next time... May God bless her... that's all I can say.

VIII
Maya

So that guy who stared at me and glued his eyes to my face will not marry me! Should I rejoice at this news or shall I join my mother and Ammalu and be sorry for myself. No! I do not want to get married and if they start with another proposal I will not agree. But my father! He will stop me from going to school just to teach me a lesson as he says. Then what will happen to all my plans to study and earn my own living?

"Why do you want to earn money?" they ask me. "Your father has more than enough. He will hand you over to a husband who can keep you in style and give you all you need. Study and earn money! Is that what you want? Do you want to look for a job as a clerk or nurse and do some dirty work all day? You don't know what men outside can do to you. Better submit to what your own family asks you to do. You will have all the servants to do your work for you. A husband is your powerful ally.. You can twist him around your fingers if you are clever enough... be always willing ... never say no to your husband."

One had to get up early in the morning on school days. The school is at least three miles away from the house and the only way to get there was by foot. There are no buses plying through the village and there were not even rickshaws to carry people around. One could ride a bicycle or hire a bullock cart, but school children always had to walk carrying their books and tiffin box. It was not difficult, of course, for young children to walk the distance, they either ran all the way or chatted with friends and never complained. They did not even wear shoes or chappals. They were ensconced in their own world and often reached the school much earlier than when the classes started.

The school had not even opened when I reached there. Peon Venugopal, that decrepit old man, who acted as the peon took his own time to open the classrooms. When the main gates opened I ran inside and put away my bag hanging it from a tree trunk. I was running alone around the building when Nanu Sar arrived and shouted for me.

"Maya! Why do you run like this early morning? Have you nothing else to do?

"I have finished my homework, sir."

"Come and sit with me here. I will ask you some questions."

He took me by the hand and made me sit close to him. I did not like his nearness and started to wriggle in my seat.

At last when Venugopal went up the steps to the veranda and rang the gong it was time to get up and go to the class.

Confusion and disorder was everywhere as we entered the classroom. Ink splashed on the seats, messages scratched on the desks, some pushing and shuffling before the teacher finally arrived waving a stick which he carefully kept by his side.

The teacher for the first period was none other than Nanu Sar. This same man who had just tried to fondle my cheeks sitting near me was a different person altogether in the classroom. He waved his cane in threatening gestures and walked up and down the classroom like a tiger in the cage. The students sat with their eyes glued to his moving cane as he went on pointing to the different parts of a map that was hanging from the wall. The map was that of the human body (it was a Physiology class) and as he pointed to reproductive and excretory organs, the girls could be seen covering their faces to hide their blushes and sly smiles.

Our Geography teacher entered when once again the school peon had almost wrestled with the gong to produce a booming sound. Apu Sar carried a stick under his arm and used it only to point to the different places on a multi-coloured map of the world. A pale young man with sideburns and a long moustache, he made us all dream of new horizons and filled us with a sense of adventure and anticipation. Although the map looked crumpled and was almost in tatters due to frequent handling, it was the one item that everyone in the class cherished and looked upon as knowledge. Those vast oceans winding their way around the globe decked in blue, those dark crazy lines that stood for mountains and the pink lure of unknown cities acted as welcome emollients on cramped souls. "That is where I *would* like to go," I often mumbled to myself as I looked at the different colourful locations." That and this and this too ... and America, of course!"

Absorbed in the map and the dreams it brought, I usually kept quiet in my Geography class. But I liked to quiz: Mr Pillai, the English Teacher, when he started his drills on Grammar. Mr Pillai, short and corpulent, could be barely seen as he stood at the edge of the table a little too high for him, except for his bald head peeping out like a shiny ball and his teeth like two fluttering rows of jagged pebbles dyed in vermilion (no wonder since he chewed so much!) His torso remained out of our sight behind the table as he laid his heavy thumb on verbs, defined their different forms and asked the class to repeat whatever he said in a loud chorus similar to the temple chant of a hundred Brahmins on festival days! And I would dare to ask him a question in the middle of all that!

"Sir, why are there so many exceptions? Can we not have just one rule to change all verbs from one tense to another?"

Before I had finished the question, Mr Pillai almost jumped on me and put me down.

"English is a foreign language," he said aloud, "The rules can be changed only by those English people as they please. They are ruling our country and I am telling you what's in their book. Why bother me with all your questions? Learn whatever I tell you!"

"Is not Gandhi fighting the British now?" I wanted to ask him under my breath. "Why should we accept all that the British say?" But I dared not upset him again with my questions.

I had heard of Gandhi and his struggle against the British from Mr Kurup, our History teacher. A young man in his middle thirties, Kurup was well read and alert to whatever was happening in our country and the world. He often spoke excitedly of the freedom struggle going on in the distant parts of the country although its rumbles were seldom heard in the small Kupam village where we lived. According to Kurup, the freedom struggle was a fight that went on between the white devils from abroad and an Indian sage in a loincloth who wanted to bring freedom to our masses. But the people in India were divided against each other due to their different castes, classes, languages and religions and could not fight together to get their freedom.

"We should forget our differences," Kurup exhorted, "the rich should share their wealth with the poor and *try* to overcome the barriers of class and caste. Have you ever heard of what Gandhi and Nehru have done for the country? They threw away their princely wealth and went to jail. They stood face to face against British bullets and are still fighting on. There are many in our country that are poor and deprived and they do not know the meaning of freedom. We have to fight and share our wealth with them." Kurup always concluded in a triumphant note.

My heart always started thumping, whenever I heard Kurup, with a strange sense of thrill and excitement. I waited eagerly to have a word with him after class or at least to catch a fleeting glimpse into his eyes. I devised cunning ways of waylaying him and plying him with questions for more information. I asked him to lend me some of his books for extra reading and also to help me join the freedom movement.

"Why do you wear those costly bangles and golden chain?" he asked me once. "One should do away with these feudal ways of living and showing off one's wealth."

"Feudal? What does it mean, Sir?"

He just smiled at me then and walked away.

When I went back home I met uncle Venkatesh sitting on the veranda looking at a newspaper. I found a seat by his side and asked casually, "What does 'feudal' mean, uncle?"

"Who told you that?" he bounced back.

"Oh! It is just a word Kurup Sar was using in one of his lessons. I do not know its meaning."

"That scoundrel Kurup? That communist rascal who turns the heads of people? Is this what he teaches you in your class?"

"No, no, uncle... he just used that word once and never explained the meaning. What is a 'communist', uncle?"

"The less you know about these, the better. I will have a word with your father about what you learn from school."

Ayya Sar who taught mathematics was of a different timbre altogether. Standing tall and straight against the front wall inside the classroom he looked piercingly at us through his black rimmed spectacles. He wore a mundu trimmed with jari on its border and used a long cane to point to the figures he wrote and erased on the black board every now and then. I was almost in a daze as I listened to his volley of words and I started rubbing my hands…

A pleasant odour of mangoes and jasmine was coming from the middle of my right palm. I could hardly resist lifting my hand and smelling my palm again and again… the smell of overripe fruits, flowers and flesh overcame me and took me to a dreamy state …

Ayya Sar was hammering on his lessons and I lost touch with his loud voice. Perhaps, he was *now leaning on the high creaky chair behind the table and rolling his luminous eyes.* Suddenly he took his aim at me:

'If 'a' equals 2 + 3 and 'b' equals 2 - 3 what is a + b multiplied by a - b?" he asked me.

I stood up with my palm on my nose and fumbled for an answer. How the old man fumed and fretted then and fetched his heavy stick and struck hard on my knuckles again and again! "That's for not listening," he said, "and for doing your own things while the class is going on."

I bore the lashes stoically and refused to weep or show any other form of weakness. Then when I unconsciously raised my palm again to my nose, the whole class burst into laughter.

Ayya Sar was a frequent visitor to my house. He often came on his way back from school to talk to my mother and at times to my father. He was spoken of as a distant relative with agreeable manners and considered a reliable source of information on the school.

As I walked back home that evening with my classmates jeering at me and repeating some algebraic equations to remind me of the lashes I had received, I turned around to find Ayya Sar quietly following us. The girls, when they noticed him, fell silent and ran away.

At home, all the children, cousins and elders had assembled in the front porch. In the middle on the floor lay Ganapthi rocking with convulsions and foaming at his mouth. It was a peculiar illness Ganapathi got every now and then and the children crowded around him whenever he got into a 'fit.' He was much older than all of them, almost an adult, although his limbs and flesh quivered with a trembling motion like that of an infant. He could barely sit up steady, and had to be fed by his own special servant.

Generally he was quiet and made efforts to smile at everyone, but when he got into one of those fits, he had to be helped by others and prevented from biting his own tongue. They even poured a bucket-ful of cold water on his face and body to make him quiet during a 'fit'. It was said that Ganapathi was a first cousin of the family and he had no one to look after him. They tried to get him married to a girl who would look after him, but Ganapathi would get a fit whenever a girl approached him. The children loved to watch Ganapathi's movements until one of the servants managed to steer them away mumbling, "My God! What a Karma!" KARMA... KARMA... KARMA! that is how the servants mumbled whenever Ganapathi got ill and it reminded me of Ramunna always saying GUAGUA ... GUAGUA ... GUAGUA. Just like the words,'FEUDAL' and 'COMMUNIST', the word 'KARMA' also began to resonate for me with strange and baffling implications.

Was it KARMA that compelled people to act in peculiar ways? Ganapathi foamed at his mouth and his flesh quivered due to his KARMA, Ammalu lost her husband and became our cook due to her KARMA, all those untouchables who always had to stand away from others and cover their faces with umbrellas made with palm leaves were born so due to their KARMAS! Then what about an old uncle of the family who had been confined to another house since he was supposed to be mad? He was not allowed to keep any money with him since he always threw it away or tried to buy something foolish. He was about to buy an elephant once and said that he wanted to ride on it! His wife, poor thing, managed all his affairs and looked after him. But she was always in tears and rued her own KARMA! I have also started wondering whether I will be also affected by KARMA and be made to do things I do not want to.

As I wandered alone into the kitchen garden where I could pick some cucumbers nestling among the creepers and smell the coriander leaves for their strong and pleasant aroma and stare at the long green chillies that looked like daggers carrying so much venom, I heard familiar voices coming from the front room. I took a turn from the garden and entered the front room to find Ayya Sar sitting there talking to my mother. He seemed to have told my mother what had happened in the class, how he had to beat me with his cane and how I had carried on as if nothing affected me. He now gave me a pleasant smile and took hold of my hands.

"Is it paining now?" he asked, "I don't like to beat you, but why are you so distracted always? If you are mindful you can be very bright indeed." So saying he raised my hands to his mouth and kissed me on the very spot he had struck. I pulled my hands away from him and rushed out.

IX

Ammalu

I like to gather these children around me and tell them stories. I have only stories breeding within me. I have stories instead of my own flesh and blood to grow and nurture and call my own. But I shall impart my stories to these children and nurture the glow on their rosy cheeks and shining eyes.

My own story, for example, how many times have I gone over and over the happenings in those years and enhanced their grip on my life at every turn ... got married at twelve to a husband who had already four children (his youngest was barely 9 - the poor lamb had lost his mother and I was to take her place). I served my Lord and Master to the end of his life, which as it turned out, was only two years after the marriage. He was the kindest man I ever met and my mind seethes with memories of those days which weave themselves into many tales as I go by.

And all those tales from Ramayana - stories of Rama, Sita, Lakshmana and Hanuman instilled into me from the time I was born ... have I not seen those stories come alive and unfold before my very eyes as I lived through them... did I not shed my tears with Sita and wait for my Ram to take me away from the prison ... well, he will not come to me in this life again, but surely I wait for him in my next... have I not waited for him faithfully all these years? And how often had I begged and pleaded like Savitri with Yama himself in those two years to grant a few more years to my husband!

Since then, I have sought my shelter in Ram's house... another Ram, of course, called 'Valya Sarni' who earned his kingdom by dint of his own hard calculation. He came from an unknown village and held his sway over this. He was black as a devil, they say, but whatever he touched turned into gold.

Then he even took for himself the pale hands of a golden girl (people still wonder how much he bargained for her!) who lay by his side for eight long years to produce five children - four boys, all spitting images of himself, and a girl, pale, lemon-coloured like her mother, her face glowing from a distance for the whole village to peep at and be ravished. The old man guarded her like a treasure chest until he found for her a young man, silent as a lamb, to take care of her along with the loads of gold and jewels he showered on her. But what a pity! She produced no issue to inherit all that gold!

"AMMALU! AMMALU!... where are you? Are you daydreaming again? Are you in the storeroom?" "Yes! Yes! I am just saying my prayers!"

Well, I pray to God every moment of my life since I got married to a husband with a terminal illness. Gods have appeared before my mind in several forms and garbs, and I have prayed to them all. Oh! What gifts had I promised to all those deities resting in our temples with shapely eyes, short limbs, and pouched bellies! I had gone round and round those stone figures with closed eyes and pleaded with them to keep my husband alive. I took several vows holding on to my marriage chain and made offerings even to those dark forces of devils and destruction to appease their jealousy ... Oh! Gods can be evil too... don't I know that? they could not brook my happiness ... they did not save that sick and pale figure enthroned in my heart in spite of all my gifts, all my pleadings ... he kept coughing up ounces and ounces of blood...blood congealed to a thick phlegm until he was snatched from my arms.

I do not pay my obeisance at the local Ganapathy temple any more... that elephant God is the favourite of the rich who keep him strong and well fed. Now I tend to share my faith with the dispossessed. I offer secret gifts to our folk deities and follow their secret codes of worship. Whenever the children fall ill (which is often), I try to persuade Saras to arrange for some black rites to be performed by the local man for folk deities. It is often risky to get this done in this house since Sekhar is no lover of black magic or voodoo. He sneers at all these matters of faith since he has had an English education. Once, when little Balu, poor thing, was having high fever and a fit of convulsions, I got a live cock through Velu and brought it into Balu's room to rotate it three times around his bed before rushing off to hand it over to the voodoo man waiting outside. The cock was supposed to carry away the evil pestering the child and when the voodoo man killed the cock in sacrifice to the deity, the child would be cured, they said. But as I was rushing out firmly gripping the cock by its neck, the bird managed to let out a desperate cry and this was heard by Sekhar walking near the gate. However, thank God, before Sekhar could actually find out what was happening, I had vanished with the cock.

"Ammalu! Arnrnalu!"

"That's Saras again! Let me go to the kitchen."

X

Maya

Morning of another day. I stirred in my bed and noticed that Meenu was already up and busy helping in the kitchen. I could hear a rumble of loud noises coming from the kitchen as if someone was being arraigned and scolded. I at once got up and peeped through the kitchen door, and was caught in a whirl of excitement that ran high among the servants there. Ammu, the woman who washed the clothes and cleaned the dishes had been once again caught with a silver spoon she was trying to hide inside her clothes! That woman, everyone had known, was a thief, and whenever she got a chance she stole spoons or saucers, or at times, even a towel or saree that she was to wash and dry! And when she was caught red-handed, she let out a barrage of excuses interspersed with loud tearful cries as to how hard she had to work and how everyone was bent on making false accusations against her! She could be heard now saying again and again,

"I have to work from morning till night! I work and work till the shit from my stomach comes to my mouth! Do you care? What will I do with your spoon? Why should I take it? Who has spread these lies? Oh! God! Oh! God! Save me!"

She was in tears now, that thin emaciated wreck of a woman, and whoever blamed her for stealing those small items was made to look like a villain in the midst of all those people who gathered around. Then, Ammalu Athai came forward from the assembled group and tried to persuade all the others saying:

"Since nothing is lost so far, why do you make all this fuss? She has not taken away anything. Leave her alone, leave her alone."

But the matter did not end there with the cook's conciliatory words. My mother, Saras, happened to arrive at the scene just then, and Ammu ran to her with a loud cry.

"Amme, Amme," she shouted, "I do all this work for you and see what these others do to me. They call me a thief after stealing the things themselves. What can I do? Would I ever take anything that belongs to you?"

Saras was in no mood to investigate the matter, she simply said, "You go and finish your work," and dismissed the group.

I had the whole day to myself since it was a holiday. As I was about to slip into the woods beyond the back yard, my father caught me loitering and thundered at me. "Where are you off to? To climb the trees? Do you pull out all those mangoes from the trees and chew them? I have some work for you. Have you heard of Bhagawat Gita? Now here is the book. Learn numbers 10 to 15 of the slokas from chapter 12 by rote and find their meaning."

He walked with me back to the verandah and a heavy book was thrown at me from his table. "Be ready to answer my questions in another hour." He then took his seat near the table and watched me turning the pages.

I tried to read the lines as given in the text. Although I could read the Devnagari script, I was not able to follow the meaning of what it said. "How could I find the meaning of all this?" I wondered. But the fear of my father's wrath hung over me like a Damocles sword. I had to learn by heart all this mumbo jumbo without a pause and find its meaning. But soon I found the meaning of those strange words in English translation just beneath those lines. It was all about what Krishna had said to Arjuna (I now remembered the stories told by Ammalu! How enjoyable were those compared to the hard task I faced now!). I read aloud Nos 13 and 14 of the slokas and paused over their meaning:

> *"advesta sarvabhutanam maitra karuna eva ca*
> *Nirmamo nirahankara samadukha sukhaksamai"*

Does it mean that joy and sorrow had to be accepted in the same spirit and with the same composure since there was actually no difference at all between them! How could I ever accept that? How could anyone? How absurd! I sat crouching over the text wondering how one could ever accept tears and laughter in the same vein. Could I ever accept the taste of delicious berries in my mouth as equal to a fall from the tree and the subsequent bruises? Never! The old clock in the verandah was ticking off seconds and minutes and soon the hour was struck. I looked at the old easy chair in which my father sat and read the newspapers. The newspaper was there covering the chair, but it was lying limp without an active, solid body to hold it up! So, he was not there! He had this habit of roaming here and there within the large compound, looking at the cows in the shed, gargling, coughing, spitting, scolding the children and ordering the servants. It was a good chance to escape from his vigilant eyes, and so putting the book carefully aside, I disappeared behind the bushes.

It was not the wild berries that now called out to my appetite; I went towards the cashew nut trees and climbed on to their easy branches. Ripe fruits brownish red, conical in shape with a fat belly to which was attached a greyish, kidney shaped shell that enclosed a delicious nut! What troubles one had to take to get that nut out of the shell! *First screw the whole shell out of the succulent fruit (be careful not to spoil the clothes in that spray of bitter juice!}, gather some leaves under the tree to hide those shells and set fire to the leaves. When those shells crack in the heat with a spurt of shell oil, keep far away since it can burn one's skin. Then when the fire dies you search for the cracked shell amidst the cinders and carefully knock them against stones to get the nut out!* Oh, what a delicious taste to eat them slightly burnt and warm! I got so engaged with the cashew nuts, stuffing them into my mouth and chewing them that time sped away unawares to late afternoon. They must have looked for me during lunch ... but I knew that I was no longer hungry.

As I returned home through one of the back doors always kept open, I could hear the furore that was going on in the dining room. Balu, my youngest brother, was crying aloud and nobody was trying to pacify him. Even Ammalu was keeping away from him and I suddenly felt impelled to rush to him. Then I could see that the boy was being punished by none other than our father himself who stood there in front of him with a threatening gesture. I tried to duck and escape quietly from his presence, but he had seen me! "Where did you run away, you bitch," he addressed me, "Have you learnt those slokas?" "Yes, father, I have. I will recite them tomorrow," I said and ran away to my grandmother's room. The grandmother was my only refuge on such occasions; she was my father's mother and he had learnt to cool his temper in her presence. The old woman was sitting in her room counting the beads of her rudraksha chain and reciting the names of the Lord. She emanated a strange sense of peace in that house which was often afire with excitement, and I readily went and sat by her side. After some time, dark clouds started gathering in the sky, and ribbons of lightning threatened to slap the eyes of those who dared to look outside. As thunder rumbled and heavy rains poured from the skies, the old woman gave me a tender hug and pulled me closer. Next she would give me some of the sweets she kept for herself in her room and I could relax in the comfort of her affection.

But I could never sit quiet for long. When the rain stopped and the golden light of the evening sun awash in raindrops poured over the green tree tops and a warm earthy smell suffused the humid air, I ran outdoors and joined the other children. They were all sitting on the open verandah facing what was known as 'puthampera' - a new block of building put up exclusively for men folk away from the din and bustle of the old house. One had to cross an open pathway of more than 200 steps to reach this new building - this 'men only' area where women and children were seldom permitted. As the children sat watching something in the open, Meenu from the kitchen joined them with fresh news and rumours from the village.

"A horrible incident has taken place today," she began, "You know that man called Paddu, who has several areca nuts growing in his yard. He had set up a trap for thieves by mounting some open knives on his trees, but he did not whisper a word to anyone about it. Today his own son climbed one of those trees and his chest was cut to pieces by those knives! The boy fell down all bleeding and Paddu's wife, the boy's mother, was beating her chest and weeping. Paddu had gone away somewhere and the poor woman was nearly crazy before she could find some help. Oh! What an unnecessary suffering!"

"How is that boy now?"

"He has been taken to Karapatty, ten miles away. Maybe he will die before he reaches a hospital. And you know what they did to stop the bleeding? They collected cobwebs and clay, and spread it on his chest. They tied up the wound with their 'lungis'."

"When I become a doctor I will help such people. They do not know what to do when accidents or diseases descend upon them," I said, coming out with my own future plans.

"No, Maya, you will never be a doctor. They will get you married before you can complete your studies."

"No! No!" Maya yelled for all to hear. "I will never get married."

XI

Ammalu

The grandmother is always the first in the house to rise in the morning. She usually went to bed after an early evening meal and was up even before the crows and the cocks began their morning serenade. It was as though her limbs, wearied during the day, spurted to new life after a good night's rest. After her ablutions, she lighted the lamp and started reciting parts of Ramayana she had learnt by rote.

I usually get up soon after and squat in front of the kitchen stool to churn the curds that was kept to set in a large pot during the night. Between the recital and the churning of curds, we talk to each other and exchange news and views. There is much common ground between us as two widows living as part of a joint family.

"Ammalu," Manni addressed me this morning. I was indeed like a niece to her and she often spoke to me on whatever weighed on her mind. "How does Saras control her children? She has a child every two years and she is hardly able to manage them."

"That is why I am here, Manni. I look after the children, all of them. That youngest Balu, of course, gets into fits at times when he is not carried by his mother and Sekhar threatens him as he did yesterday. Poor chap! His nose was running and he was weeping aloud to be allowed to sleep with his mother. He hankers after his mother's milk, but it's a pity ... Saras has hardly any milk to give him after she lost her latest one..."

"Well, we have to feed him with cow's milk ... we have enough cows and cow's milk." Manni started reciting again and I stopped my churning to peer into the curds for clots of butter.

"Give me a dollop of butter, please," pleaded Maya as she entered the kitchen. She was also one of those who woke up early with a head full of unruly ideas. She took her seat close to her grandmother.

"Maya, you are no longer a child," I said, "Eating butter will make your breasts grow bigger. Your father will have to find a groom for you sooner."

"Oh! No," Maya asserted, "eating butter has nothing to do with marriage. Is it not so, grandma?"

Grandmother pretended not to hear her query and asked her, "When will you finish school?"

"I shall never finish," Maya answered pertly, "at least until I become a doctor."

"A doctor ...? You can more easily become a mother than a doctor." I quipped I could see that Maya was quite upset by what I said. She ran away from the room without a word.

XII

Maya

Every one around me has such a bleak and ordinary picture of my future. Even Ammalu and my grandmother think that I am just waiting around to get married. For the elders in this village a girl child is like a calf to be sold and sent away to another house. My plans to study and join the Freedom Movement are dismissed and sneered at... no one takes me seriously. But if I were a boy like Ramunna, I would have been sent to college! Somehow I would also like to attend a college after my school and when Ramunna comes home next time I will ask him whether there are any girls studying in his college.

But what shall I do now? Shall I go and meet Kurup Sar and ask him how I can join Gandhi and Nehru in their work? Can I get their addresses so that I may write them letters? I need to think and plan now.

I decided to take a walk by myself and look at the way the poor lived in their small shanties away from the main road. Children with running noses were playing all round those little one- room tenements thatched with coconut leaves. Coconut trees and several other plants and herbs surrounded these homes. The people around were surprised to find me wandering around those places and asked me where I was going. "Where is Mala's house?" I asked, "Mala? That girl who is in some trouble?"

"You cannot see her. Go back home." As I was trying to walk back home through several alleys and bye-lanes I came across Kurup Sar carrying a small baby and walking towards the market. He seemed embarrassed on seeing me and asked me what I was doing there. "I am just looking at the poor people," I said.

"Why don't you teach them to live better?" he asked and walked away.

Meenu joined me when I had reached the main road. "Where did you go?" she asked.

"I was trying to find Mala's house."

"Yes, let's go there. I know where she lives."

We had to go through several small lanes slush with cow dung and slippery mud and go over narrow footpaths partially hidden by brambles before we approached an opening barred with bamboo poles tied at the ends with coiled coconut fibres. We jumped across the bars which came up only to our waists and reached a house with a low thatched roof and an open verandah. As we tried to climb the steps leading to the verandah, two hefty men, probably Mala's uncles, stood in our way and shouted, "Go Home, Girls!"

We could see a vociferous group of people in the inner room assembled around a prostrate figure with her face to the wall. She was lying there as if in a fit of convulsions (almost like Ganapathy?), a spectacle of abject misery howling with acute pain.

> *Mala! My dearest friend, how have you come to this... her incessant desperate sobs had sent desperate shivers through my spine and I stood there numb with grief The group around her were her own family members... her father who had always been nice on earlier occasions had a grave and forbidding look now ... her uncles stared angrily at us, her cousins and aunts had covered their faces* in *their shame and grief. They all had surrounded Mala's body and I suddenly noticed that they were smearing her eyes with a green paste. She screamed every time they approached her and they shouted abuses at her. "Shameless slut!" they shouted, "Shameless slut that has brought such dishonour to our family. You think you can get away with this? Tie up her hands! Let us see how far she will go." I was aghast at the scene I witnessed and looked around for her mother only to find her at last in a corner weeping inconsolably. A group of all and sundry including servants were clustered at a distance and there was a hush-hush of whispers going round I noticed that what they were trying to apply to her eyes was indeed a paste made out of green chilli... those Kerala chilli that looked like daggers, full of venom that our servants ate with a mound of rice and tapioca. This was the torture designed for Mala by her own people and the reason for it all ... no one dared to say aloud. Mala had just turned fifteen*

> *and she lay there trying to turn her face to the wall to avoid their onslaught. Suddenly someone asserted "She will tell! Give her a sample of that chilli paste right on her eyeballs and she will shout the name of that scoundrel who brought us such shame. WE will tear him to pieces ... don't we know where to hit him, tear him to pieces and break him to pieces?" Some one hit Mala on her back and pulled her hands. They all tried to break into that cordon of grief, children screamed and women sobbed as the guardians of morality advanced with chilli paste* in *their hands.*

'They will not let us go near her," Meenu said as I stood there as in a dream, "They are torturing her and trying to get the name of that boy who has brought her to this. But she won't tell"

"Go home, Girls," that was another shout to shoo us away.

On our way back home we had to pass by the corner shop that often served as the nerve centre of the village for the locals to hang around. The shop was carved out of the narrow jutting front of a typewriting school that prepared the village youth just out of school for any clerical job available in nearby towns. Adjacent to the teashop was the local post office that was kept open only during afternoon hours since Subramania Iyer (a Brahmin) who served as postmaster had to double up as priest during the morning hours. But his priestly chores seldom interfered with the postal work since the number of letters he had to deal with in a day hardly came to more than twenty, not to mention those days when he drew a blank with no letters at all. The village had no more than 200 families, most of them illiterate, who had never heard the rustle of writing paper or held a pen or pencil.

That entire building block with the typewriting school, post office and the corner shop stood in full view from my house when the gates were open. In fact, the whole building was owned by my father who had leased it to the post office. I had the full attention of people standing around whenever I passed by and they often giggled and tried to pat me on the back.

Now they were curious to know from where I was coming and whom I had met.

"Hey! Aramperannol," they addressed me as usual, "where are you coming from? Did you go to meet your Kurup Sar?"

When I refused to answer, they slyly looked at me and asked, "Did you tell your father where you were going?"

I made haste to run away from them without a word. I had been often cautioned at home against talking to 'such' people that gathered around the teashop and it was always safe to run away from them. There was hardly anyone in that village to equal the power and wealth of my family and no girl from our family was allowed to move about or talk to common people.

XIII

Velayudhan

Velayudhan is my given name ... Velu for short. Night and day I watch over this big house and perform all the biddings, big and small, from my masters and their women folk. I know all the corners of this big house in which I have practically grown up, clinging to my mother's mundu as she worked here from dawn to dusk, cleaning clothes by beating them against that large block of black stone near the well. My mother, Amni, used to rush to the big house every morning with me nestling against her ample bosom and sucking greedily from her open juicy breasts. Those days are gone now ... She is also gone... So too my father whom I have seldom seen although he also worked for 'Valya Sami' as his right hand man helping him to build his vast empire of land and gold. They say that our world is changing now, the days of 'Kali Yuga' are coming close to breaking the old order we were born in. But I don't know how it will affect me ... a poor man who has nothing to call his own other than his loyalty and hard work. No one taught me how to read and write, but I see and hear everything that goes on around me. I read people's faces as they try to tell me many things I don't understand.

I worship at the temple of Bhadrakali, the ferocious consort of Lord Shiva who wants to barter her favours in return for the blood one can spill in her honour. And I am always ready to spill my blood for my Goddess and receive her blessings. I decorate her temple with blood-red banners and red hibiscus (as red as her own tongue always sticking out in warning!) and I keep vigil inside her temple on festival days fasting and chanting her innumerable names. Then on special nights I join the bare-bodied youth of the village in scanty loin cloth and hoist myself from an iron hook (specially provided for the purpose) and hang from the ceiling until the blood from my loins drips to the floor in front of the Goddess. Then as the crowd surges to watch us faint and drained, the hooks are lowered to let us lie prostrate at the feet of the Goddess. Then if the mighty Goddess is pleased with our sacrifice she deigns to enter our body and possess our tongues to utter her prophetic words ... That is where my loyalty takes me and that is how my world is built!

But now I can hardly understand what is taking place in our village and why.

Unexpected events are happening and certain evil thoughts are allowed to raise their ugly heads out in the open. Well, I am thinking of whatever happened yesterday just in front of the post office near our big gate. Kottakudi Sridharan, that local rowdy, picked up a quarrel with our temple priest cum postmaster! He accused that revered Brahrnin steeped in chants and mantras all morning of not delivering a money order due to him! And the postmaster, Subramania Iyer, a high caste Brahmin who wouldn't even touch a paper addressed to low caste chaps like Sridharan washed his hands of all responsibility and said that he had received no such money order. Then, of course, you can guess what followed! Hard words, flinging words of abuse from Sridharan not only for the postmaster, but for the entire high caste Brahmins for all their tricks and plots against the low caste poor.

"Stealing my money, anyone's for that matter, is nothing new to you and your kind. All the 'pattars' like you in the village live on the poor and build big houses. Is it only that government salary that is keeping you in such splendid idleness? (Pattar was an abusive term used in the village for high caste Brahmins!)

The postmaster got really flustered ... his words got stuck in his throat... he used his voice only to chant mantras, but now how could he find words loud enough to put down that ruffian?

That was when Sitaram, the postmaster's nephew (an aspirant to his uncle's office after his retirement) entered the scene and the crowd gathered. Sitaram has a sharp tongue as everybody knows.

"You are a menace to our settled life," he shouted to Sridharan, "You roam around doing nothing and you pilfer whatever you get. You are a threat to our women and girls. How dare you accuse a government official? You deserve to be HANGED!"

Sridharan's rage rose beyond control at this stage. Hurling out all the abusive four letter words in his vocabulary (there are quite a stock of such words in local parlance) he flew at Sitaram and caught hold of him by the neck and was about to knock him down when Sitaram produced a sharp cutting knife (usually used for cutting vegetables!) and dug into Sridharran's stomach. Sridharan fell down bleeding, there was much hue and cry and two policemen, often loitering around looking for trouble, arrived on the scene. Sitaram was caught, handcuffed and sent to jail while Sridharan had to be taken to the hospital at Kottapady. He was eventually declared safe and when Sitaram was later released from jail on count of self defence, all the Brahmins rallied around him and turned him into a hero! "How can that rowdy ever think of accusing our priest of a non-delivery of a non-existent money order?" they chimed together. "The menials in this town are really getting cheeky! We should teach them a proper lesson."

How could such an incident happen in our quiet little village, I wonder! As I stood there mute at 'Valya Sami's' gate watching Sridharan fall down bleeding and Sitaram being handcuffed by the policemen I felt the world had gone topsy-turvy!

Ammalu, as always, wanted to know all about the fight outside the gate. She, as a woman (and a widow to boot!) is not permitted to witness such rowdy scenes (although she manages to find some peep-holes!)

"Velu, Velu!" she called me to the kitchen soon after and spoke in whispers, "what was that commotion outside? Please tell me!"

"Just a fight between Sridharan and Sitaram! You know how those two are always itching to fight."

"But why? Did the police come?"

"Yes, Sitaram is arrested and taken to the jail for killing Sridharan."

"What? What? Please tell me! How could Sitaram, a good Brahmin boy, spoil his hands murdering a Chovan like Sridharran?"

"It is not caste that started it, Ammalu! Subramania Iyer failed to deliver a M.O. due to Sridharan and then the quarrel started. Sitaram interfered with a kitchen knife he was carrying."

"Oh! Oh! Whatever is happening to our village! We had so much quiet here, but now all those Chovans and Nairs will be boiling with rage against the Brahmins!"

"But, Ammalu, I am a Nair and you are a Brahmin. We are not fighting. Do you think all of us will be stupid like Sridharan and Sitaram?"

"Velu, we are what we are only because of Valya Sarni! He made the rules and we obeyed. But now that he is gone, will the rules be followed?"

"Stop it, Ammalu, when Kali Yuga comes, even an earthworm will ooze out venom! Even you and I may change when the time comes."

As I watch the cows being lined up in their shed for feeding and milking, I start thinking of the good old days under the iron rule of 'Valya Sarni'. Once when one of his errant tenants, a Chovan by caste, refused to pay his dues 'Valya Sarni' had ordered my father to set fire to the thatched hut in which he lived and pull out that shifty Kochunni by the scruff of his neck like a fox from his hole, but no one - not one of the Chovans or Nairs - in this village dared to raise his voice against the landlord or use that derogatory word, 'pattar' against the Brahmins! But, now any little thing is enough for a flare-up... we are living on a pile of cinders ready to catch fire.. when Chovans and Nairs fight against the Brahmins who own this village... where will I find my place? I owe my flesh and blood, my life and my soul to this one family and my fate is always linked with theirs.

XIV

MAYA

We had another class in History and Kurup Sar was really great in the classroom. He went on and on about Gandhi's struggles against the caste system and the fight for independence. The rich should share their land which belong to the poor, he said. The Chovans and Nairs have the same blood as the Brahmins, he said, and that untouchability was a social evil. Most of the class sat listening and asked no questions.

I followed Kurup to the teacher's room after the class. There was no one else there as I talked to him brimming with new ideas.

"I am really excited by what you said today, sir and I want to work for the elimination of the caste system. Could you please give me the name of the book you were reading from? Can I borrow it from you for a day or two?"

"I have got it here. I can also give you some others which will help to clear the cobwebs in your brain."

"Cobwebs, sir?"

"Yes, in the sense that your mind is blocked now with no avenue for action."

"You are right, Sir. Please tell me what I can do. I want to learn Hindi ..."

"Go to Vasudevan Nair. He can give you private tuition. But you have to pay him."

"I have only some gold chain and bangles, Sir. No money ..." "Give all those to me. I will settle with Vasudevan."

So that is how I have now settled it with Kurup Sar. I handed over all my gold ornaments to him in exchange for arranging my Hindi lessons. I could also borrow from him several books to bring me dreams and visions of a different kind of society in which authority could be resisted and questioned. Land and wealth were to be shared with the poor and the land-less and even women could participate in social reforms on equal terms with men. The old shibboleths of people around me were the 'cobwebs' to be cleaned and done away with by ushering in a new world.

Kurup has arranged a meeting for me with Vasudevan Nair. The meeting is to take place tomorrow in Nair's house and I cannot tell this to anyone in my home. I have to be quite secretive about my going to a Nair's house and I have to pretend that my gold chain and bangles are in the cupboard.

Mondays and Thursdays after my school I sneak my way to Nair's house and learn my Hindi lessons. Nair says that if I learn my lessons well I can become a Hindi Pracharak for the Freedom Movement. I feel excited and impatient to start on my own ... Maybe I can travel to distant places to teach Hindi and even one day hope to meet Gandhiji in one of those places! But now I have to lie about where I was spending my time in the evening. But I suspect that Ammalu is closely watching me. She asked me today why I was late from school. "I was with Sita, Ammalu," I said, "playing hopscotch."

"But, you know, Maya, your father does not favour your going anywhere after school."

"Please don't tell him, Ammalu Athai," I said and gave her a big hug. "When I grow up, I am going to travel around and you can come with me."

XV

VELAYUDHAN

A heinous act had been committed last night and it has rattled the whole village and sent chill shivers of fright and terror down the spine of everyone. The local temple of Ganapathi has been vandalised and desecrated by unknown villains and the village is rocked with fear of divine punishment. Who could have done such a deed in our age-old temple where hundreds of Brahmins and devotees pray and chant every day to reach out for the blessings of the mighty Elephant God!

Early this morning, the priest Subramania Iyer had woken up his little servant boy, Iswar, and sent him with the keys to open the temple, before he himself took his early morning bath and changed into a clean loincloth to do his puja in the temple. However, Iswar came running back from the temple with a cry of alarm and despair and could hardly make himself clear while spewing out a stream of words that indicated that the temple was already open and its sanctum sanctorum vandalised and polluted by unknown miscreants. "My God! My God Ganesh! Whatever has happened to you! Whoever has done this to you?" so went the cries of Iswar as he tried to tell the priest that something terrible had happened inside the temple. Subramania Iyer decided to rush to the temple putting off his plans for a bath and change of clothes only to find himself swept off his feet when he saw the atrocities done inside! It looked as though a pack of godless demons had broken the lock and entered the temple in the dark hours of the night and polluted the entrance and the corridors with rotting rubbish and human excreta. They had also combed around for valuables and made away with the tall brass lamp and golden decorations of the idol. Whoever in our God-fearing village could have such guts to offend and pollute the village God! It was quite unthinkable what they had done. Iyer stood in front of the idol and begged forgiveness by reciting some mantras and set to work without giving much publicity to whatever happened. He asked Iswar to bring buckets of water from the tank to clean the place and contacted one or two helpers to wash the whole place. When early morning devotees came to the temple they could see what was being done and they all joined to help. This incident has shocked everyone in the village and rumours are adrift that those low caste fellows disallowed from entering the temple had been emboldened to do such a heinous act. "Those accursed ones are losing their sense of place," they said, "they have been incited by these ideas of running after freedom and they have indulged in such sinful rebellion. We shall guard our village deity. He is sure to punish them in his own way."

It was Sekhar who called me early morning and asked me to go to the temple to assist in the cleaning-up. "Take all the soap and brushes you need," he said, "Tell them that I have sent you." I ran to the temple, but hesitated at the door from entering the sanctum sanctorurn (I know that I am a Nair and so allowed to worship only from a distance). Subramania Iyer, on seeing me, waved and endorsed my entry and I set to work along with others to bring back the dignity of God to our village.

Ammalu was all agog when I returned. But I had to report to the master first who heard everything and mumbled almost to himself very gravely, "The Gods are to be protected these days from the people... See what is happening with all this talk of freedom and equality." I did not quite grasp the meaning of what he said, but I knew that he was really worried.

The village has got into a frenzy of guilt and fear after that incident. Several rites of purification and atonement are to follow, and even some of us from the lower castes who worshipped elsewhere, spilling our blood for the appeasement of fearsome deities, want to stand around the Ganapathi temple and pray before the placid Elephant God. I don't think our master Sekhar ever went to a temple, but he is sure to give a big donation. And the police? Although the priest had duly reported the loss of valuable items from the temple, our police are seldom able to trace anything lost, or find any clue leading to the culprits.

As the summer keeps dragging on to reach its extreme peak, most people stay indoors keeping their windows shut to bar the sunlight. The sweltering heat before the monsoons makes them distraught and they lie on cool cement floors fanning themselves with palm leaves. But my work takes me into the fields and stables and I walk about the vast rooms keeping watch. Who knows what will happen next in this God-forsaken village? I find that Ammalu and her team are always at work in the kitchen burning firewood and churning out several dishes for all the family. Ammalu makes no complaint about the heat unlike the others, but rushes to the well to dab her face every now and then with fresh water. She always asks me something or other whenever I cross her path.

XVI
Maya

I know that I now have to keep a thicker veil of secrecy about my Hindi lessons and the visits to Vasudevan Nair's house. After what happened in the temple and the increased tension between Brahmins and the lower castes, everyone is anxious and watchful. I skip the last class at school to get more time for my Hindi classes. I always find some pretext or other for leaving school early.

I find it very interesting to spend time in Nair's house. In fact, he told me that the house was his wife's and he was only a guest son-in-law! What he meant of course (as he explained later) was that according to Nair customs different from those of Brahmins, man marries into the woman's family and stays there at the pleasure of his wife. This was indeed directly opposite to what happens among the Brahmins who marry and bring the girl to their house to keep her there at their will and pleasure. Nair wives have therefore more freedom and rights than the Brahmin women who are always overruled by their husbands. Vasudevan Nair, in spite of all his learning, always looked weaker and submissive in his wife's presence. He had many goals and ideals to realise, he often said, and these included freedom for the country and full equality for everyone. I could float on a stream of new and fanciful ideas whenever I was with him.

I could discuss many of my ideas and future plans with Nair. He gave me an idea of the extent of divisions and differences within our society. "We all belong to one country," he said, "but we have so many different traditions. We must learn to tolerate as well as integrate these different traditions. That is what Gandhiji stands for." I asked him why in his Nair tradition women seem to enjoy more freedom and power than Brahmin women. I told him about Ammalu who lost her husband when she was so young and had no place or wealth to call her own. "There are so many social, economic and political reasons for such situations," he said. "We have different Gods and Goddesses and so different reasons." "Is marriage the only vocation for women?" "No," Nair said, "Women marry according to their wish. Nuns in Christianity do not marry at all. Marriage is not compulsory." I wished to tell him how marriage was the only option available to me for my future since my people did not allow any other, but I felt ashamed to admit so much in his presence.

One day as I was going towards his house, I came across several buses and cars plying their way through our narrow and wretched village roads. We rarely experienced such a sight in our village since very few outsiders or vehicles came our way. Nair told me later that many tourists were passing our way in order to go to Kurusumudi where a stone had been found bleeding by a farmer as he dug the soil. This was indeed very strange and immediately the news had gone round to bring so many people rushing to see the sight.

"They have taken it as a sign from God," Nair said, "but which God? Hindu Gods do not bleed and some of them demand our blood as sacrifice. Now they have found a God who was bleeding (whether it is blood or some similar dye nobody knows), and the Christians have claimed it as their God who actually died on the cross for the sins of humanity. The Christians immediately wanted to build a church on the spot while the Hindus thought they could fit in Shiva, the God of Destruction, on the bleeding idol. People from all around are rushing to the place which is on the top of a hill and they have to pass by our village."

"Which God could it be? What do you think?"

"I am not superstitious. I don't see God in a stone."

It really surprised me that such an extraordinary event should have happened in our quiet village and I wanted to go there and see for myself. But I was never given a chance to do so, although some of the servants in the household managed to visit the bleeding idol.

During bedtime on one of those nights, there arose a near commotion in the children's room. As Balu got ready to get into his bed and opened it (the beds were usually kept rolled during the day) a large frog was found crushed and stuck to the sheets. Balu started howling and raising a hue and cry, and all the children assembled around him. That poor thing, the frog, had come inside to hide and escape from the heat, and had been crushed inside the bed, but Balu was scared and refused to sleep on the bed. When Arnmalu arrived on the scene to console him, she told him that the frog had come only to tell us of the coming monsoons and it will soon take a new life to sing for us during the nights. She then threw the smothered creature out through the window and replaced Balu's sheets. As I witnessed the scene and heard those consoling words of Ammalu with regard to the coming monsoons and new life for the dead frog, I felt a new surge of hope for me and my future. "Isn't there a God behind the veil of nature," I wondered, "who really cared to bring faith and hope for those in misery?"

Late one night when almost everyone had floated into a state of slumber under a pall of pitter-patter from the rain and bouts of thunder, muffied cries and sudden screams for help were heard from the kitchen. Rudely awakened, almost everyone including the servants in their dens, rushed to the kitchen where the doors were open with gusts of wind and water pouring in. Ammalu was lying on the floor with her hands and feet tied, and making those desperate cries for help. The intruders, whoever they were, had left without leaving a trace. When Athai was finally able to speak she said that she was still washing the dishes in the cool of the night with the doors open when suddenly two rogues with black visors had entered and knocked her down. They then tied her up and tried to molest her even as she struggled to make her mute cries. "But they could not do anything," she said, "they ran away when you all came."

"Did you recognise them?" Velu asked her.

"They had covered their faces, but I could hear them talking in Malayalam."

My father came in now from his room with his big stick and asked everyone to go back to their beds.

"Why the hell did you keep your door open?" he shouted,

"Why do you keep awake so late in the night? There are all kinds of rowdies in this place now waiting for a chance. Keep quiet about what happened today."

But more shocking news came out in the morning which could not be hidden from the public. The same set of rowdies who had tried to bring disgrace to my house had also struck at another house - the house of one of our distant cousins. There, the widow of the landlord had lived with her sons and she had been hit brutally with a heavy weapon, and much gold and currency had been taken away from her cupboard. Those rogues had found their way in by cutting the window bars of a room instead of walking easily in as it happened in our house.

The sensational revelations of this case totally engaged and took the breath away of everyone in the village - including the police who came from Kottapady next morning. The general conjecture was that these rogues were none other than some disgruntled tenants who had been provoked to an act of rebellion against the rule of 'pattardom' in the village. The village physician tried his best to revive the wounded widow and record her oral statements, but to the horror and shock of everyone, the poor widow never came back to consciousness. The case was registered as burglary and murder and all the Brahmins who had prided themselves as landlords now trembled in their shoes.

XVII

VELAYUDHAN

AMME! A:MME! MAHABHADRAKALI! I cannot believe whatever is happening in front of my eyes! You are my only solace and I have to accept that YOU have ordained it all! How can anyone dare to come into 'Valya Sarni's' house and threaten the cook? How can anyone have the courage to murder the landlord's widow? These are terrible times, more so for Old Faithfuls like me who do not know the world at large... I have lived so far in my own little world always ready to obey my Lord and Master. But now, some people in this village are even trying to poison my mind by pouring hidden stories from the past into my ears! They tell me that 'Valya Sarni' was a ruthless man who took away the wealth of the village from the poor people and built his own mansion. He exploited everyone, they say. And they whisper into my ears the most terrible of their falsehoods that makes me tremble, "Velu, Velu," they say, "You don't know who your real father was and who you are. That "Valya Sami' took advantage of your poor mother who worked all day long in his house. You should have rebelled against what he did to your mother rather than be his slave. Did you get a portion of his wealth? Did your mother get any? You, stupid fool! Join us and claim your share!"

I know they spread this rumour all around gossiping in the teashop and it churns my mind. Amme! Amme! My divine Goddess, help me for all the blood I have shed for you!

XVIII
Maya

Everyone around me here seems to be in a panic. They seem to be sure that there will be many more incidents of the nature that took place, but I don't believe them. I want to go on with my studies and Hindi lessons and I want to join the Freedom movement. We cannot live in fear always.

Yesterday Vasudevan Nair asked me whether I would like to accompany him to attend a gathering of Hindi scholars and students. It is to be held next Saturday in the neighbouring town at least five miles away and the participants would have to be away from home at least one whole day. There was also to be a procession and slogan shouting against the British rule before the conference. I really wanted to go and attend this conference and meet all those people who I felt sure would think like me and will be my friends. But I cannot inform anyone in the house about this programme and so I quietly slipped away hoping that I will not be missed.

I joined the procession and offered to carry the flag in front. I also learnt to shout slogans which were all in Hindi. The conference gave me a chance to know the names of various places in India where Hindi was spoken as a mother tongue. When it was over around 6 p.m. I started walking back home with Nair. I was quite tired and hungry and was not in a mood for a long walk. Nair tried to keep me entertained by asking me several questions about my study plans. At some point when the road turned out to be full of ups and downs and it started getting dark Nair asked me to take his hand. I was not used to holding hands, particularly with grown up men, and so I drew back from him. But when I was about to slip and fall over a stone, Nair grabbed my hands and continued to support me. It was indeed an odd feeling, holding a man's hand, and leaning on him, and I shuddered to think what people back home would say if they came to know.

When I finally reached home, it was quite dark and as I jumped over the gate to enter the house as quietly as possible, I was suddenly confronted by my father pacing up and down the veranda.

"Why are you coming so late? Where were you all this time?" shouted the old man.

"I have been to my Hindi teacher," I replied.

"Your Hindi teacher? Who the hell is he? What business has he to keep you there? Who gave you permission to go for these lessons?"

It was then like hell let loose with the old man's shouts and uncontrolled wrath, and all the others in the house started gathering to watch the stormy scene. My mother then came out with all her stored up complaints about me: my not wearing the chain and bangles and talking about the fight for freedom. My father had got so furious by then that he took hold of my hands and slapped me on my burning cheeks several times. "Next time you go to see that vagabond, you will see what I will do," he shouted and pushed me against a wall and was gone.

I retreated to a dark corner of the house in my pain and humiliation and tried to hide my tears when my brothers and sisters came to peep at me. When Ammalu came calling me to the evening meal I refused to go. Later mother came more to admonish than to console me

"How can you go with that Nair for a whole day without even telling me? When did you start going to him? Your father was right in punishing you. Now you go and have your meal." I kept quiet and followed her to the dining room.

I could hardly get any sleep that night even after all the others had gone to bed. As I lay there tossing the leaves of my numerous doubts and fears I became aware of a faint conversation corning from my mother's room next door. My mother usually slept alone with her infant-in-arms, but tonight I could hear that she had someone else with her engaging her in intimate whispers and strange movements. As I strained to listen, I could hear the gruff voice of my father in an uncommon low pitch:

"I have to do something about that girl very soon,,, he muttered, "How have you brought up that girl? Have you told her why girls get married? Have you told her about this ...?"

My mother was giggling and turning around in the cot for some reason at this point and I wondered at this strange reaction from her. "I have done everything I can," she said. "She does not listen to me.,,

"You have given birth to so many girls. You should know how to deal with them.,,

"Oh! I am sorry! I am ashamed of her ... she is a curse on me... she is running after some strange ideas taught by her teachers. If only we can arrange for her marriage!"

"You very well know what happened to your cousin in Palghat. They engaged a tutor to coach her for the exam and the girl got pregnant before the exam. That bloody Nair ... the tutor ran away after that ... How can my daughter go to that Nair's house for Hindi lessons? That Gandhi mania is catching on even in our village and our own girl is getting involved. What are you doing as a mother?"

"Oh! I don't know what to do. I can only look after them when they are small ... the older ones hardly listen to me.,, I could hear her sobbing as she said this.

Tears welled up in my eyes as I listened to my mother and I wished I could make her happy. But I also knew that it was impossible for me to give up all my ideas just to please my parents.. Can they not try to understand me and help me realise my desperate need to be free and help the country? Maybe it was my ego that created such desires in me, but why should I suffer by denying myself?

My Hindi lessons were discontinued from the next day. I was told that I should never again try to meet Vasudevan Nair. They questioned me on the gold ornaments I had handed over to Kurup as fees for my lessons and my father got furious and abusive. He said that all these teachers were just a pack of thieves who took advantage of me, a stupid girl. He summoned Ayya Sar and discussed the matter with him. Finally I was told that Ayya Sar had certified that I knew all my lessons and so there was no need for me to attend school. I might appear for the final examination if I was so inclined.

The village postman who rarely visited the house now started making frequent appearances. He brought letters addressed to my father which were smeared with turmeric and I knew these letters had something to do with exchange of horoscopes and marriage proposals. Were they again trying to get me married, I wondered. One day my mother called me aside and told me that we were soon to be visited by the parents of a boy who was being considered for marrying me. I should carry myself with modesty and charm, she said, and I should learn to prostrate before them respectfully and answer questions without moving my lips too boldly.

"All the talking will be done by your father and me," she said with great motherly pride.

"Look what we are doing for you. We are doing our duty as ideal parents. A girl is the property of another house and the parents are to take care of her only until it is time to entrust her to the rightful owner."

I could not suppress the sense of hurt and humiliation in being thus treated as if I had no choice at all in deciding my future, and so asked her with a sense of annoyance:

"Is it what you are going to do with me? You two brought me into this world and made me feel constantly guilty for being born. And you wouldn't allow me even to complete my schooling. You wouldn't allow me to do anything on my own ... you plan just to hand me over to someone else. I will never agree to marry ... I cannot."

"But, it is not anyone, Maya. It is one destined for you and we find him through matching horoscopes. And do you know, this particular boy we have chosen is from our own family ... You will have everything if you agree to marry him."

"What I really want is to have my own choice, mother. Can I have my choice in this marriage?"

"You don't know what you are talking about, Maya. You have to obey your father." She walked away from me with a flourish and turned back again to tell me, "You better learn some cooking from Ammalu. Also a few songs to sing and please your new family members."

Left to myself I sat brooding over my fate. I felt at that moment that I could despise all married women I had seen around me. They were all mostly stupid, carrying on their servile life, with no voice of protest. I could not understand how even my mother who went around so quietly had reconciled herself to such a fate. Did she want to make her daughter's fate similar to hers? What did she feel years ago when she was brought to a stranger's house as an infant bride - she was only ten at that time - and left to lead a life of quiet submission.

As I sat there brooding over the sad plight of all married women, Ammalu Athai peeped in from the kitchen and came to sit in front of me and put her arms around me.

"Maya," she said, "marriage is not such a sorry state to go into. If you have a kind and good man as your husband, you can be very happy and fortunate. You will just love whatever he wishes you to do and you will have lovely children. Please agree to get married as your parents wish and trust in God to find you a good man. After all, it is your own Karma that determines your fate."

I quickly disentangled myself from her embrace and looked at her with my eyes full of defiance. "You are talking of Karma and stopping me from doing anything. Are you sure that I will ever get a chance to study and do what I want to do with my life if I now keep quiet and agree to marry whomever they choose? I will only be confined to the house and bound by so many rules and restrictions. I want to be free, Athai, and I want to fight for the freedom of our country."

"Nobody can be totally free, Maya. This world is a sea of 'samsar' and we are all bound hand and foot to stay in it. It is your Karma from the previous birth that determines your fate now. How can you ever hope to be free? You have your family, caste and particular character and these will not allow you total freedom. Will you be happy without your own family and social position?"

"I don't know about all that now. All I know is that I don't want to get married now."

"Well, you are only 12 years now and you have to follow what your parents say."

She went back to the kitchen to get herself busy with cooking, and as I looked at her I wondered whether she really wanted me to get married like she did years ago. When her husband died soon after leaving her alone, she had to take up cooking in somebody's house and put up with all the trouble with only those far-away looks and 'day dreaming' as my mother called it. If only Athai had a chance to study and be on her own, how much happier she would have been! But she never had that option and so she came to accept whatever came her away.

However, there were still several dark questions that confronted me with regard to women and their dependence on men. All the girls I knew were happy to get married and they seemed to entertain several glossy notions of their life after marriage. Were they just looking for a comfortable life to be provided by the husband along with a lot of gold ornaments and costly dresses? Or were they really attracted to boys for those secret reasons that they told each other in subdued whispers? Since I did not share such feelings with them, I had put away all notions of marriage and considered it only as a strategy for denying me my freedom and hindering my dreams and plans for the future. I had not yet become vulnerable to any sense of attraction for the opposite sex and considered marriage as only an exit strategy planned by others.

Next day the village music teacher, Samu Bhagavatar, arrived at my house along with an urchin carrying his harmonium. Velu made haste to spread a mat on the floor for the maestro to sit down and cross his legs to assume his performing style. The urchin left the unsheathed harmonium on the floor in front of the teacher and Ammalu got busy fixing a cup of coffee for him. Soon I was brought and made to prostrate before him as a mark of respect before sitting down to learn my first lesson.

"I just cannot sing, master," I managed to say. "My throat hurts and I produce such hoarse sounds."

"Sit down quietly, little girl," he replied, "Just listen to me and you will feel alright."

Then he started tuning those strings of the harmonium for what seemed a long time and harped on one of those long and winding ragas which went on and on as I sat there and quietly watched the rhythmic contortions of his body and facial muscles that added a visual dimension to the auditory nuances of his melody.

These music lessons, however, continued only for a week. Samu Sar thoroughly enjoyed playing to his captive audience and filling the landlord's house with rich renderings of different musical chords until one day, my father arrived on the scene quite unexpectedly. The maestro went on with his raga hoping to mesmerise the landlord and add to his entranced audience. But my father had no ear for music and he boldly intervened and shouted above the sounds of music. "I don't think it is necessary for Maya to learn all these for getting married. I can find a groom for her without all this ceremony of a sing-song." He turned to my mother who had just come in and added, "Do not trouble our Samu Sar with all this. Arrange to give him a suitable gift and let Maya alone from all these lessons."

But I was not left alone for long, since my mother got busy pushing me for the next step towards preparing myself for the forthcoming event She wanted to get some gold chains and bangles made for me and she called a thattan (goldsmith) to take my measurements. I refused to meet the thattan and protested saying that I was neither going to wear any gold chain nor get married.

"What do you mean?" my mother asked me in alarm. "How can you disobey your parents?"

"I only mean that I want to pursue my studies and not get married." I replied.

"But we have fixed up everything for you. All of them are coming to see you."

"But you never asked me before fixing up. I have told you long ago that I do not want to get married."

My mother's face turned black and blue on hearing me and she ran to my father to give him the shocking news. She was really agitated and almost burst out saying that it was a curse on her that her daughter brought up in a distinguished family had refused to obey her parents.

My father was sitting in his armchair thinking of the various arrangements he had to make for the marriage and the amount of money he would soon have to spend as dowry, gold ornaments and gifts.

When Saras broke in with the news, his first reaction was one of casual dismissal of the problem. "Send her to me, will you?" he said with authority. I was then summoned to his presence and he almost jumped at me.

"What is this nonsense your mother tells me about you? Did you say that you wouldn't marry the boy I have fixed up for you?"

"I only said that I don't want to marry now. I want to study," I ventured to reply.

"Silly girl!" he shouted, "Study! What is the use of all this study? All that a girl needs to study is to count two and two and write her name in her own language. You may need to sign your name in case a house or property is transferred to you by your husband! Better get married into a decent family. Do you think that I am here to provide for all your study and nonsense? I want to get rid of you as soon as I can. If I chuck you out of the house what will you do?"

I suddenly wanted to cry and started wringing my hands. I wished that my father had taken a milder tone so that I could have told him how I really felt and how I wanted to do some service to the nation when I grew up. I might even be able to earn some money, I wanted to say, and repay him for whatever he spent on me now. After all, I was doing well at school and could even become a doctor. But my father had no patience even to listen to me.

He just shouted at me, “You better do what I tell you. You don’t know how it is so difficult for a girl to live without getting married. Someone will make you pregnant and you will be in the streets begging.”

“I do not want to marry, whatever you may say,” I brought myself to say, much to the irritation of my father.

Don’t you want to have a child of your own, girl? How can a girl have children without a husband? Do you know what happens between a husband and wife?”

“I don’t want to know any of that,” I insisted.

“Aha! Then I will teach you what happens when you turn against your own parents,” He then turned to the people gathered around him and shouted, “Velu! Velu! Bring two long green branches from that mango tree.”

I started trembling. I knew how terrible my father could turn with an onrush of wrath. He could strike with all his might until the victim was totally silenced. I remembered the last occasion he had struck me with his hand for coming late. Now he was going to strike me with a raw cane. When Velu brought the cane Sekhar got up from the easy chair almost regally. “Show me your hand, Impudence,” he said, “Don’t think I will take all this nonsense from you.” My hands flinched even before the volley of blows came down. Something was happening in my head which made me look at my own hand and the scene around me as a dream. I could feel the pain and hear the lash as if it all happened at a distance. I could see my mother rushing to the scene and wiping her eyes with a corner of her saree, I could see Velu and his brood looking on with incredible surprise. I could see the twitching of veins on my father’s dark forehead as he fixed his eyes on my extended hand receiving blow after blow. I was too dazed even to cry, but I managed to keep standing with a tremor travelling up and down my body. Sekhar finally stopped in triumph and said, “You will be careful next time you talk to me.” He threw away the cane and walked into his room.

But that was only the beginning of those terrible days. After my father had thrown away the cane and withdrawn to his room I continued to be in a dazed state and retreated to a dark corner, sitting still for a long time. I could not understand what was being done to me. I had only wanted to study and achieve those goals which were deemed great and heroic by everyone. Why did the teacher say that Gandhi was a great man? Why did so many join the freedom movement and exhort others to do so? Will I not be allowed to participate in any heroic action although it was all that I wanted to do in life? To get married to someone whom I had not even seen, (can just seeing make any difference, I wondered) and to lead a life of drudgery which I saw around me every day ... was that all I was allowed to do? Should I just help my father to get rid of me from the house? How can he threaten me so and even beat me to make me submit blindly to his commands? I could not comprehend the meaning of life in those terms. Suddenly I wanted to die then and there and I started weeping bitterly. *Death, Death Death,* I repeated to myself in between sobs, *what was it after all? That one would cease to exist when one dies and then no one could lay his hands on you any more... That they would burn the inert body and reduce it to ashes, wasn't there another world where one could enter without one's body...* I kept my eyes closed as I tried to visualise another world.

However, I persisted in my refusal in spite of worse threats and punishments. My mother pleaded with me with tears in her eyes, but I simply turned my face away. My father would come every now and then with loud shouts and curses, even flog me again and ill treat me, but I persisted in my refusal to obey them. Yes... those were terrible days of suffering, but I would not give in to blind obedience. I became almost a pariah in the family with the servants trying to rebuke me and the children ridiculing me. Even when I was with my own people I felt that I was in a strange far off country full of icy strangers who looked at me with mistrust and suspicion.

But I was also learning something these days... to think about my body as something different from myself and to encourage it to endure pain on my behalf. The concrete aching body could be observed and contemplated on from a distance by a consciousness that lurked around on a close watch. *Is that what happens when one dies? Will the soul hover around an inert body?*

Thoughts of death and afterlife came to me unbidden and I vainly searched for a God to whom I could pray to end my misery. But what will happen to all my plans for the future if I were to die too soon?

XIX

Velayudhan

In the sacred name of the divine Goddess whom I worship every day of my life I can swear that I have not seen so far anything like I am seeing today. A grown-up girl in 'Valya Sami's' family refusing to get married and her father beating her in front of everyone! Not once, mind you... almost every day ... and she lives her days of agony dipped in tears, but putting on a brave face! What she does is wrong, I can agree; she should obey her parents and pray to God for giving her peace. But how can she be treated like this, worse than a slave or animal! Amme! Goddess! Forgive me for doing what I did ... he ordered me to get the birch from the mango tree and I cannot say 'no' to him ... I am only a servant after all... if I had refused, someone else would ... and I will have to swallow all the abuses from the Sami (I have never said 'no' to him ever!)

They are all trying to advise that girl, but she would not relent. She has the family blood in her to fight and overcome ... the father's blood in his child fighting with the father himself... how will it all end ... We have to keep a cover on all these happenings ... if anyone outside comes to know, the family will come to shame... A gloom has spread over our daily round ... we go on hoping for the best and praying for divine grace ...

XX

SEKHAR

I cannot understand this... I cannot understand this slip of a girl from my own loins ... she is adamant, self-willed and conceited... she does not trust her own parents... she wants to take control of her life... chase that stupid dream of Gandhi to reinvent our society and our lives! He would not have had this dream but for the British ... he should be indebted to the British for recasting his mind with new ideas, but he uses those ideas to discredit the British. The British brought many blessings to our country, we live on the fruits of their administration and education... I do not want the rabble to take over the country by claiming a share from everything under the sun... But my own daughter wants to chase these foolish dreams and upset our family name ... She won't listen to reason... I have to crack the high whip on her ... but her defiance amazes me.

My mother and wife are now always after me asking why I have been so rough with her. And they also keep complaining about her, her refusals and disobedience! What can a man do when he is caught in such female tantrums?

"I want to break her pride," I tell them, "I will see that she comes down to obey me like a dog," I say.

"But we cannot drag her unwilling to the marriage pandal," my wife reminds me, "If she does not marry willingly the bridegroom's party will pack and leave," she adds.

"I will make her all right before that happens," I assure her.

I feel as if my nerves are taut when I am reminded of her obstinacy. I walk around the house almost looking for a confrontation with her. And I find her now seated at breakfast and staring at her palms where I can still see those livid marks inflicted by me.

"Do you still persist in your idiocy? I ask her challengingly.

"I still want to continue my studies," she says almost defiantly.

I could no longer control my fury, my rising ire against this 'problem child' in my own house. I took hold of her with both hands, gave her a kick with my foot and pushed her down. I could see her struggling with her mouthful of breakfast and waves of uncontrollable sobs, but I just wanted to get away from the scene. Let the others help her to get up.

XXI

Maya

Oh! This is death ... I am now going to die ... I can neither swallow nor breathe ... he wants me to disappear ...I have just been thrown on the floor with my mouth full and I cannot gulp down or breathe ...

But my heart still seemed to beat... in fact it is rocking against my sides in wild agony, but I was dumb and stricken. Ammalu came then and helped me spit it all out in bouts of vomit and I sat up on the floor. I knew that I was not dead. What shall I do next to get away and find another life?

Two days later, my father summoned me to his room to talk to me. He wanted to reason with me, it seemed, and there was no threat in his voice. He addressed me as gently as he could.

"Maya, What can you ever hope to gain by disobeying me? I will never again send you to school and you will have to live here as a menial until your brothers and their wives decide to throw you out. Do you know what will happen to you if there is no husband to take care of you? Just think what happened to Ammalu and Mangalam even when they were safely ensconced in a family. You have no idea of whatever a man can do to a woman. Foolish girl! Women can never be alone and free. But if you get married, you can persuade your husband to let you do whatever you want. He might even let you study."

He then stopped a moment to snigger as if he had just made a joke. 'I know that trick of yours,' I thought to myself and then replied,

"I know he will not let me study. I have not heard of anyone who did that after marriage."

"But I will make a contract with him at the time of marriage," he said, "He shall certainly let you complete your studies in school or at least as a private candidate. You don't seem to know your father's power in getting things done."

But I could not trust him after all that had happened between us so far. He had been so severe and harsh with me so far that I could not bring myself to believe in him. He would only try to entice me in a trap.

"I don't want to marry. I only want to be free."

"There are no free women in this world," he almost shouted in reply. I could see that he was beginning to lose control over his voice. "If you find any free women, you may be sure that they form the scum of society. Do you want to be one of them?"

I knew that our discussion was over as he quietly walked away and shut the door to his room.

I did not see him again for a few days. Then one day, my mother came to me with tears in her eyes."

"You don't know what you have done to your father. His nerves are under severe pressure and his hands are shaking. He walks up and down his room without any food or sleep. He curses me for bringing such shame on him and his family... and he even moans and cries in shame for himself ... Maya! what a monster you have turned into! Have you no love for your family? For your father and mother? God will punish you, Maya, for thinking only of yourself and your foolish goals."

"Mother, I am very sorry if I have hurt you, my father and the family. But you only want to send me away. I do not even know which God you are talking about. There are so many Gods and they are all so different. I am helpless. Can you not help me grow and do whatever I want to do?"

"When you don't know what to do, can you not at least obey your elders? Why do you have to be so defiant and conceited as your father says?"

I could not find any words to reply to her. Instead I tried to go closer and hug her in our joint anguish. But she walked away from me saying, "I am ashamed of you, I cannot understand how a child of mine has turned to be what you are."

I accepted her words as a slap on my face and shed my tears alone.

I decided that I should now try to leave my home somehow and seek shelter elsewhere. I wanted to find out how I could join a boarding school and continue my studies. But I knew I had to contact either Kurup Sar or Vasudevan Nair to get me this information. Then it suddenly occurred to me that I could send them a letter describing my present condition and ask for their help to get me out to some girls' boarding school outside our village. When the letter was written I entrusted it very confidentially to Velu (I was sure he sympathised with me although he always obeyed my father) and asked him to fetch a reply.

I waited for that reply trembling all over with anticipation and anxiety. Two days later, Velu brought the reply and I was overjoyed on reading it secretly in my corner. Yes, there was a boarding school run by a convent in a small town 40 miles away and it was possible to get admission on payment of fees and permission from the parents. Could I talk it over with my father and get him to sign the admission form?

I gathered all my courage and resolution to approach my father as he was walking listlessly in his room. I managed to tell him in so many words how I could be quite safe in a convent boarding school with so many nuns to look after me and help me with my studies. The school was indeed so close to our village and I could even come and spend my vacation at home. And when I had studied enough to get a degree I could decide what to do next. I pleaded with him to help me.

Then, of course, the hell broke loose. My father could no longer restrain his fury.

"You... you... you ..." he shouted, "You want to join those freaks at the nunnery, worship their weeping God and go astray! You want to bring shame on my family that has always held its head high! Our Gods will punish you for this, you will be cursed forever!"

"What Gods!" I exclaimed, "Have you ever believed in any of those Gods? Have you told me to believe in them and why? You always said that these Gods were made up by men for their own use. My mother had to hide her gifts to God from you and you always prided yourself as a rationalist. May be you are right...

There is no reasoning behind having so many Gods. I refuse to give up my goal in life for some uncertain and mythical Gods"

He then stared at me in blind fury. He could not believe his ears. Who had been teaching her to say such things? How could she grow so much out of control... his problem daughter! Suddenly his hands started smiting my cheeks left and right without a pause with the full force of his weight. I collapsed at last on the floor with both my cheeks blazing in feverish agony. I had seen sparks of fire coming out of my cheeks whenever his blows came down on me. I had always noticed it when my father hit me with all his force on the cheeks... my eyes emitted sparks of bright light before coming down in torrents of rain. I ran and threw myself in a corner. I abandoned myself to a fit of weeping. It was an unspeakable agony that I suffered on that day. After a fit of violent sobs, I rushed to the kitchen and took the longest knife from the shelf. The whole troop of my little brothers, sisters, cousins and servants marched behind me, wondering what I was going to do. The knife looked so gruesome that I looked stunned simply holding it. But I rushed to my father with the knife in hand and cried, "Kill me with this knife at this moment. You brought me into this world unasked for, and you have fed me on shame and anguish all my life. Take away my life now since I don't care to have it any longer. Free, free my aching body from this terrible presence of life. You have to do it now." My voice fell saying this, but it left lasting echoes in the room. I threw the knife in front of my father and stood awaiting death as a lamb at the sacrificial altar.

Then the moving world around appeared totally disengaged from me and I could see it like a luminous globe turning around like a dizzy dancer while the blue enveloping clouds flitted past the surrounding oceans churning them with frothy caps.

XXII

Sekhar

I could not believe my eyes and ears as she approached me with that gleaming knife and requested me to put an end to her life! How could a puny girl have so much courage? How could that girl be so perverse and defiant to assume that I, her father, had anything but her own interests in my mind as I tried to arrange her future! I might have been harsh and impatient with her, but that is only what our custom demands from us. We in 'Valya Sami's' family seldom succumb to sentiments ... we want to get things done... we know how to keep our women and children in their places. But see, what is happening! Our whole world is turning topsy-turvy and this girl, the wildest of my own seeds, challenges me and threatens to make me feel like a woman wanting to cuddle her with consoling thoughts.

The thought of death had always frightened me and it has remained the last closed door on which my rational views have knocked in vain. But this girl is calling for death as a passage to the journey she longs for. I had so far seen only a perverted ego and childish obstinacy in her moods and actions and I had tried to teach her a lesson, but now I have a glimpse into the depths of her despair and anguish. I realise that she is not a mere calf I could kick and tame, something I possessed as one of my property. Had not I been wrong in dealing with her as I did all these days?

I stood for a moment stunned with awful thoughts as my wife and other children looked on at the brink of tears and weeping. The knife lay still in front and Maya was gazing at the scene as though from an extra-terrestrial corner. I kept looking at her wondering what was going on in her mind. The unfathomed depths of a father's heart rocked and rumbled within my chest and my earthly reason crumbled as at the onrush of tumultuous waters from within. The hand of authority, the hold of custom, melted away into the thin air of uncertainty and I was thrown into a realm of the incomprehensible which I had failed to acknowledge openly.

"Maya, my dear!" I finally brought myself to utter, "Who ever thought that you were so serious on studies and on plans for your future! We were trying to help you the best we knew how to, but if you are so keen on your own plans you can certainly do what you want. But you will have to arrange everything yourself and take control of your life. I can give you the formal permission you need as well as the fees required. Do not make it all an issue of life and death and create such hysterical scenes. Get up and bring those forms to me."

Since there was a general consternation and total silence on hearing what I said I decided to say nothing more.

XXIII
Maya

Yesl He said those words for all to hear. He said that he would sign those forms and send me to that boarding school where I can plan my future! Now life beckons to me with all those rosy dreams I used to struggle against.

He, my father, who I thought revelled in his authority to bring me to book and punish me stood shaking before me most awkwardly and he said that I was indeed serious about whatever I wanted. What more do I want now? Will I not now forget all those days of terrible conflict, vehement shouts and callous neglect? In the midst of strangers away from the family will I be able to make my dreams come true?

The retinue of little ones and the troop of other onlookers followed me with their eyes as I got back to withdraw to my corner.

Then followed a period of strenuous study and coaching to make up for all the time I had lost living almost in a limbo of despair and outbursts of rebellion. I was left very much alone without any active interference from anyone to prepare myself to join the school. Only Ramunna wrote to me from Calcutta giving me his best wishes. He himself seemed to be having a tough time fighting his way in a strange city and growing out of his usual boyish spirits. But I had, by now, only one goal in life: to get out of my home and start a new life.

LEAD, KINDLY LIGHT

I

Maya

I was woken up next morning by the peals of Angelus. I could hear a flurry of muffled sounds all around - there seemed to be many others around me getting up from their beds, stretching their limbs, folding their bedcovers, and groping their way to the bathrooms in the dim light of zero watt candles that had kept their vigil throughout the night. A splash of water ... a loud report from one of the pipes ... I sat up reluctantly and reminded myself where I was. I was no longer at home in the midst of several brothers and sisters in a spacious room nestling under the shade of a huge mango tree that rained its fruits, leaves and branches on the roof tiles, I was no longer under any threat or constant fear of my father... I had at last managed to escape from my cramped-up life at home and enrol myself in a girl's school run by Carmelite nuns.

I had come there only last evening escorted by Ammalu Athai and Velu, that nincompoop man, an obedient slave in his master's home, but who now looked mighty puffed up during the journey as he assumed the role of a male escort for two helpless women. Ammalu Athai was looking rather cowed down when she came out of the safe precincts of our home and I tried to remain defiant and silent, looking for a life of freedom as well as further studies that would equip me with the means to live my own life. Athai had tears in her eyes as we parted at the convent gate, and Velu almost admonished her as he hastened to take her back to the bus stop. I carried my bags to the front parlour where a smiling nun welcomed me and sent me on to a dormitory.

The dormitory was at the end of a narrow corridor after a flight of stairs. Several beds were lined up in a longish hall and several inmates were moving helter-skelter, stuffing their bags and things under the beds and talking incessantly. No one noticed me as I entered and tried to find the bed No.13

assigned to me. At last I found it almost in the middle of the hall and as I sat down for a few minutes watching others, they turned to me and plied me with so many questions. They told me that the next meal was dinner to be served in the refectory across the corridor down the stairs, a good walk away from our dormitory. But one has to go first to attend the prayers down the hall. "Are you a Catholic?" they asked. "No, you don't look like one... You have to go on to a small room at the other end where the non-Catholics are required to pray."

> "Oh! God, Creator and father of all the Universe, Father, I most profoundly thank You ..."

Thus began the prayer I had to start chanting with others in the room (all of them, non-Catholics!). A single nun clad in black from head to foot, her shining eyes peering through her white visor watched us closely as we chanted. Then there was also that monitor, a tall girl who read out the prayer line by line.

"Now, EXAMINATIO N OF CONSCIENCE," she shouted and there was a hushed silence.

"Now recall in what way you have acted against the voice of your conscience and disobeyed God, your loving Father ... Did you wilfully disobey any rule, command, or lawfal desire of those appointed by God in His place to guard and guide you?"

Then all of them had to murmur in chorus and chant *'I am deeply ashamed and sincerely sorry for having thus offended you. Turn not away from me, Pardon my sins and help me hereafter to shun all occasions of sin ..."*

The pall of silence finally lifted, they marched towards the refectory where two long tables were lined up with dinner plates. A retinue of women and girls served the food while several sable clad nuns walked around the tables overseeing all. A very tall and fair nun towered above them quietly plying a shuttle. The bustle of conversation around the tables rose and enveloped them all and reached an overwhelming pitch.

That first evening and night within the safety of the convent had now broken into the first light of the morning and I had to take my place in the line in front of the bathrooms.

Why? Why? Why had I come here to join all these people quite unlike myself to lead a life quite unlike mine so far ... to call on the help of a Father quite unlike anyone I had known or heard about so far? What nonsense was

I making of my tender life blind with cravings for an unknown frontier... to break through the boundaries set up by my own people in my own interest perhaps ... Would not the rustle of silk, the glitter of gold, vast mounds of delicious food and an array of servants to do one's bidding in one's husband's home prove to be a better option than this waiting in a line to get a chance at the wash basin! But no! Already the bell was ringing to summon us all to breakfast and to attend the classes.

II

The classes commenced soon after breakfast in rooms with different numbers in another building away from the hostel. Almost everyone who marched into the Chemistry class wanted to sit on back benches with their own group of friends and I had to take my seat on the front bench against the direct glare from the spectacles of a nun who came to lecture - a short figure of medium size scrupulously clad in white with a black veil over her head. She stood barely above the long heavy table in front of her, there was a piercing light in her eyes that kindled a glare of attention. She spoke with authority of the several basic elements in Chemistry, listed the formulae and urged the class to take notes. She concluded the class with an exhortation:

"Would any of you, any of my students, be blessed to discover a new element to add to this list? May God bless me with a genius among my students!"

She walked away at the stroke of another bell ... there was a slight tilt in her gait as her full figure came to view near the exit.

There was much gossip among the girls about Sister Ignatius (as the Chemistry teacher was called). She was all fired up with Christ and Chemistry, they said, and she had suffered from polio as a child. But Christ and Chemistry had saved her and brought her to the nunnery. Her idea of salvation came from the hope that one of her students would one day discover the 110th element and be acknowledged as a genius. "Didn't anyone try to get her married?" I asked them gaping with curiosity. They suddenly burst into a jeering laughter at my question and someone said, "Who will dare to marry her?" Then they had again started laughing almost hysterically until someone pushed me to the middle of the group. Then they had started clapping their hands and clamoured, "why don't you ask her yourself?"

Teaching in a convent school was by no means restricted only to nuns. There were also other teachers from the lay community, some Catholics and even non-Catholics, but they were all mostly unmarried women well past the marrying age according to those around. "Our English teacher was once heartbroken," one of the girls said, "She fell in love at the age of sixteen, but it was impossible to get married to her lover and so she came to the convent to study and then to teach." Another teacher was called 'a wallflower' since she was unable to find anyone willing to marry her. "Even some of the nuns here ..." another began to say, but started giggling and stopped at mid- sentence.

But I thought I was above all such nonsense of relating a woman's standing to her opportunities for marriage. Do women study and work only when they are unable to get married for whatever reason? Do all those who remain unmarried share a past of disappointment, rejection or disability? I could never accept these hints. As far as I was concerned, marriage was an anathema, a sort of bonded labour... I wanted to count my worth only in terms of my ability to be free.

It was indeed exciting to sit on the front bench and listen to those teachers who became my role models and achievers since they had managed somehow to break through those bonding social rules and stand on their own feet. Was there anything more thrilling than that to look forward to? But those enthusiastic responses and gestures from the front bench did not curry favour with one's peers. The rest of the class seemed to be allergic to such blind admiration and were quick to pounce, denounce, and ridicule. They had so many techniques to expose and jeer at one's vulnerability, they could easily turn one into a laughing stock and float seemingly-ugly rumours. They often talked of these teachers in front of me and criticised them in order to provoke me to come to their defence. When they called Miss Bose a hard-hearted spinster and a miserable loner, I told them what an inspiring teacher she was and how Miss Bose had encouraged me to think. But they had simply started laughing at me and said aloud, "You have a crush on her, don't you?" In fact I did not even know what they meant by 'crush', I only knew that they were laughing at me. Similarly when one girl asked me whether I was moon-struck, I was unable to understand what she meant. "I like to look at the moon," I replied with an unpardonable naivety.

One day, there was a sort of rebellion in the refectory. Some one had spotted a cockroach in the *dal* and there was a hue and cry. Some of the girls decided to take a protest march to the Principal' s office and put up their complaint. They picked up the cockroach and put it in a jar and as they started going, one of the girls pounced on me, placed me in front of the procession and thrust the jar with the cockroach into my hands. "Maya is a great admirer of the Principal; she will lead us to her office," they announced. Willy-nilly I was pushed to lead them and asked to state the demands of the resident students: "Better food. Cleaner food. No more insects in food." The Principal looked aghast as the girls approached and she looked up and down to identify the faces as she turned to them somewhat harshly, "This does not happen every day, does it? This happened only one day due to the oversight of one of the cleaning girls. Can you not understand? Go back to your rooms." They all quietly turned back and I felt ashamed of my enforced participation.

Miss Susan stood head and shoulders above all the other teachers: she had her swash-buckling ways when she came to her lessons in Physics. The laws of reflection and refraction assumed metaphysical proportions when she dealt with them. She could usher them to a universe beyond the tiny classroom in which they huddled together, and set them up as voyagers into mysterious spaces. But, outside the classroom she asked them too many personal questions: "Do you have brothers and sisters? How many? Do you like the food here? What do you plan to do after your studies?" She gulped down all the information with a sure sense of appetite. I was emboldened to ask her several questions about herself, but she never gave a straight answer. Sister Polydora, tall and ebullient, was well versed in all the lessons one could learn from History. The focus of her mind was like that of a searchlight flitting up and down vast chunks of information to sift it all to capsule forms readily dispensable. At times, she spoke too loudly and one could never be sure that she was quite satisfied with her students' intelligence. She was always one for authentication, redefinition and extraction.

III

Then one early morning, a girl who had just gone inside the lavatory came out screaming with expressions of revulsion. It looked as if she was going to throw up and she covered her face with both hands. "Oh! Oh! Who has done this... how did it happen ..." she cried. They all surrounded her wanting to see whatever had happened. A roll of bloody cloth had been pushed into the hole of the toilet and the flow of water had been blocked ... who had done it and when was the question. Why was it not thrown in its proper place into those drums downstairs? Soon a witch hunt was on and everyone on the floor was being questioned and carefully watched. No one came forward ... mutual suspicions ran high ... it has to be one of them...but who? After breakfast all the girls were called one by one to be questioned by the Sister in Charge, but when the bell summoned them all to the classes it was as if the event was forgotten ... no more questions ... there was a hush as they all hurried to reach their classes.

During the evening prayer and those silent moments of Examination of Conscience, that morning's incident seemed to loom large in the room. "Who, who was it? Did anyone admit the misconduct? Did anyone's conscience suffer with that non-confessed wrong doing? Was anyone weeping silently or was it being remembered only as a moment of defiance?" *"I am deeply ashamed and sincerely sorry for having thus offended you",* they chanted together and started walking towards the refectory. I was rapt in a deep pall of gloom and confused thoughts as I took my seat ... *Does anyone here know whatever I have gone through at home? Does anyone guess how disobedient I had been to my father at home?*

Then deep into the night... during those darkest hours when I lay quiet, still unable to sleep, I heard a low moan from a bed in the corner of the big hall. Was someone having a nightmare? Or was it a muffled sob? I got up and walked as though on padded feet towards that sound and stood across the crouching figure on the bed. Suddenly the girl in the bed got up and threw her hands around me. "Let's go outside the room," she said and led me to the closed door and outside. She had started sobbing again and sat down at the first spot she could sight near the window.

"Oh! Oh! I have to speak to someone," she said, "I am all stewed up within ... It's I who did that terrible thing yesterday. I was afraid to go down and throw it, but they found me out."

"Found you out! Did they punish you?"

"Punished me even more severely than if they were to beat me," she said. "They have put the fear of the God into me. I am a sinner. I wish I had not done it, or having done it, confessed it before they found me out. Now I will be watched and watched. I am restless within me. You know - what's your name? - I have so many sinful thoughts within me. I want to go home and get married ... At least then I will not feel so lonely and afraid all through the night." She started sobbing again and tried to embrace me.

I felt uneasy and shrank from her touch. "My name is Maya,"

I said, "what is yours?"

"Don't you know? I am Theresa, one of the seniors. I have already spent one year here under this strict surveillance of nuns. I am miserable and lonely here. When I came here last year they gave me a room downstairs with only one roommate. I got quite close to her and was nearly as happy as I could ... but those nuns did not like it. One night the warden took it into her head to inspect our room and found us sleeping together. 'No, no,' she said, "You have to sleep apart. You have come here to study and worship God... not to indulge in sin.' Then she moved me to this dorm upstairs where 20 girls keep watch on each other... Oh! What a soup I have landed into!"

"Where's the other girl now?"

"She was moved somewhere else... but this year she has quit her studies and gone." Theresa assumed a disconsolate face as she said this.

"Why don't you go home?"

"Oh! I can go home only after I scrape through these exams. My father says that I am a wild thing ... he wants me to be tamed by these nuns. He won't get me married until these nuns certify. He threatens to make me a nun if I disobey." Her words were tapering off to a gloomy silence.

I sat with her holding hands and trying to console. At last I said "let us go back to our beds, someone might see us."

The friendship with Theresa started thus did go to great lengths. We always went to the refectory together although we had to sit apart on our assigned places. Our classes, of course, were different, but she rushed to meet me after her class. She did not have anything good to report on the teachers or the lessons they taught. She dwelt on her own discontents and kept holding on to me. The others started noticing our growing intimacy and sneered at us. However, I was not always quiet or docile since I often tried to tell Theresa about the benefits of studies and being independent.

"Really, Theresa, your father seems to be a good man," I said. "He wants you to study so that you won't be a slave to others. How different he is indeed from mine who stopped my studies when I was just twelve and tried to get me married by force."

"Oh! he did that, did he? I wish mine had done it to me. But no force, mind you... I would have gladly married my neighbour's son who was always hanging around me... Oh! He had such handsome curls and lovely eyes."

"How old was he and what did he do? Was he in your school?"

"Oh! No, he was only sixteen and lived with his mother. He did odd jobs for a living since his father was dead. He used to come to our house to take the cows to the bulls for mating..." she started giggling.

"But why did you want to marry such a fellow?"

"Oh! He looked so handsome... and he knew ... what it was all about ... between men and women, you know." I suddenly found myself at a loss to carry on the conversation and wanted to be left alone.

IV

Then one evening, as I sat alone watching others play shuttlecocks in the badminton court, Sister Ignatius came up and sat next to me.

"How are you, Maya," she asked, "How are you going ahead with your Chemistry? Are you going to do us all proud, girl? Will you outshine all and get a first? We have a gold medal for the best student and you should try to get it."

"I shall try my best, Sister."

"But, look, dear girl, don't waste your precious time in idle company. You are here to study."

"I know, Sister."

Whenever we had those classes on English poetry the attendance seemed to be larger than usual. Not that anyone was allowed to skip classes ever without an apology signed by the hostel warden, but there were always those who had opted for Arts classes and came in large numbers. Pin-drop silence as always when Miss Jyoti, that pretty, buxom woman so tastefully dressed started her lecture on John Keats. Miss Jyoti was only a substitute, someone said, for the nun who used to teach English and who now had slipped and broken her hip. Miss Jyoti usually taught composition, but now she had been requested to take up English poetry. She went on and on over the poems of John Keats and turned on all the girls to a pure sense of admiration for Keats as well as for herself "John Keats, so young, so romantic, wrote such lovely poetry ... he was so forlorn with love... What a lovely world of dreams and desire... of Beauty and Truth etched in unforgettable words. Oh! but he died so young... he was tubercular.. what a pity! And they had no cure in those times for such disease, as we have now. And how can one explain that poison in *Isabella?* Beware of all those Greek legends and ideas that get mixed up with Keats' imagination ... his mind was not simple and realistic like that of Wordsworth. Have you read Wordsworth's *'Affliction of Margaret'* or *'Michael'?* That older poet deals with simple paternal and maternal sense of loss and grief whereas Keats was far removed from reality as simple peasants experienced it."

The class was stunned to silence during Jyoti's lecture, but there was also a lone voice of disappointment from Theresa as we left the classroom together. Theresa said, "I wish she had told us about Fanny Browne and why she rejected Keats." I was unconcerned with Theresa's disappointment since I could only think of those notions of Beauty and Truth that had so overwhelmed Keats in his poetry. I wondered how Truth and Beauty could be perceived as one unity as Keats did. Maybe they could be seen as one when one's dreams are translated to reality and if so, Keats had been able to turn his dreams to some kind of reality, I thought. Keats was indeed more interesting than Wordsworth who with his simplicity and peasant imagination did not have much appeal for me. Well, I have had enough of peasants and their grief in and around Kupam, my own village, where I lived in those miserable years.

Classes in moral instruction were held for non-Catholics when Catholics had what was called Catechism. (I never understood what was meant by Catechism!) When Theresa went to attend her Catechism, I went to my moral instruction classes. These classes were engaged by Sister Stella, a sure-footed nun with a marvellous facility for words and quotations from books. Her only objective was to instil in us a sense of God and of real happiness, and she was intent on proving that one was impossible without the other. She said this again and again with much conviction and used exemplary images and quotations to prove her point.

"Are you happy?" she questioned them, "What is happiness? You may say that you are happy, but then you will start thinking what else you need for completing that happiness. If you are aware of God you would not need anything else: your happiness will be complete."

She was certainly different from other teachers since she stopped lecturing at least ten minutes before time to invite questions from the students. Once in her class I put up my hand and asked "how do we know there is a God?" (memories of confrontation with my father had assailed me as I said this).

"Think of all the great men and thinkers of this world," Sister Stella replied in an assertive tone, "They have all searched and found God. You have only to look into yourself to find God, my dear girl! Read all the writings of saints and great teachers and the God within you will respond."

"But there are many who are quite happy without God," I insisted. "For them doing the things they want - eating, drinking, playing and earning money -bring happiness."

"Is that what you think?" Sister turned to look at me piercingly as she replied, "they are not really happy, my dear girl; you can take it from me that they are only pretending to be happy, chasing one thing after another. Only God can bring them real happiness. "That assertion rang through the hall and the day's session came to an end. I left the room feeling quite at odds with myself

My question, so boldly addressed to Sister Stella in the Moral Instruction class seemed to have made me more visible to everyone. All the nuns looked askance at me afterwards and the girls started teasing me for bringing the nun's way of life into an open question. In fact, I had been impulsive in bringing up such a question and it was assumed that I was critical and irreverent. Theresa pounced on me as soon as we were alone and told me that she loved the way in which I had questioned the nuns. One day as I was waiting outside the teachers' quarters to submit an answer sheet, I heard my name being mentioned and commented on by those within. "That girl, Maya, is one of those doubters who has nothing but problems," said one of those teachers.

"I wish I could talk to someone and unburden my doubts and fears," I told myself and walked away with strange misgivings.

V

Days and weeks plodded on in a series of tasks, breaks, meals, prayers, classes and examinations. I never lagged behind in my studies, although the results did not place me at the top. I had always more questions than answers.

Then one morning, hell seemed to have broken loose in the hostel. One of the girls living in a double room downstairs was being arraigned with questions as she stood weeping disconsolately. The warden and the Principal had arrived and she was being escorted to the Principal' s office even as her things in the room were being packed and taken away.

"What happened to her," everyone wondered, "what was she guilty of? Where was her roommate? (No girl was allowed to live alone in her room). But no one came forward to explain anything to the girls who had gathered around. In fact they were being shooed away to go to their rooms and get ready for their classes. The Principal gave them all a sullen look as she returned to her room. I could see that she was holding on to her rosary with her clenched fist.

The news came in bits and pieces and whatever came thus had no stamp of authenticity with each one coming up with a slightly altered version ... was there a true original version at all? The real facts relating to the incident seemed to have escaped them all and I thought that they were all trying to build around the usual love story and its aftermath to explain away the incident. The girl's roommate had gone home on leave to attend to her ailing mother and the girl had spent the night alone, it was said. Then it was whispered around that she spent the night with a boy whom she had invited to come to her room scaling the convent walls. "How could anyone manage that?" they all wondered. It must have been a boy with whom she regularly corresponded. But were not all letters censored by the warden? It must have been someone she just met at the gate while going to church ...but how could she do that considering that they were always escorted by two stalwarts whenever they went to the church? How could she ever dare to do such a thing! Was it all just a trumped up cock-and-bull story just to scare the girls? No rumours were allowed to leak beyond the hostel walls (what a bad name it will bring to the convent!) Finally it was all made to look as if she left the hostel and went back home for personal reasons. No one dared to say that she was guilty and was expelled from the hostel.

The life of routine asserted itself once again. There were also some special days when the girls celebrated the Feasts of Saints whose names some of the Sisters had taken. There were efforts to cut and paste special greeting cards for Sister Ignatius when they all went together to greet her and she exhorted them to work hard. On the Feast Day of the Principal special items were served at the Refectory - they had fruits, sweets, and even a special *dal,* not the usual watery broth that went by the name of *dal.* The Catholics were escorted as a group to spend long hours at the church while the others were allowed to say their prayers quietly as they wished. I walked alone around the campus since Theresa had gone to the chapel along with others. This close friendship with Theresa had already caused me much embarrassment and I found myself brooding on it as I sat alone. Theresa was leading me to a new kind of intimacy that I had never experienced before. Back home none of my brothers and sisters were so excited about being close to me and touching me... in fact, no-one other than my grandmother and Ammalu Athai had shown any special interest even to listen to me... I had always gone on a different wavelength away from all the others. When Nanu Sar and some others tried to stop me and hold my hands I felt uneasy and tried to free myself from their grasp. I remembered with a shudder the last occasion when my father had tried to hold my hands after having beaten me black and blue and driven me to desperation. No! no! I cannot allow anyone to touch me and hold me to submission... Now Theresa was just coming to that ... she wanted to sleep in the same bed with me and rub my body. She was holding me up with all sorts of sob stories and preventing me from reading books and making use of my time to get to the top. Besides, Theresa seemed to be unhappy and critical of everything that went on around her and she made me feel inadequate about going ahead and making my own plans. Didn't Theresa often tell me that she 'loved' me? That word 'LOVE' from what I had associated with it so far raised more questions than answers and made me uncomfortable. Was such 'love', whatever it was, permitted to be displayed in front of all the others? Or else why did Theresa or even I feel so guilty and secretive about it before the others? I could not totally deny my own responses to Theresa's overwhelming overtures nor could I fully approve of them.

VI

I received very few letters from home. My mother occasionally scribbled a few lines in the native language to say that they were all well and to ask me how my studies were going on. I received my monthly cheques signed by my father with no covering notes or best wishes. It had been agreed that I could go home for the vacations 'if I felt like it.' Christmas vacation was still far away ... at least three more months, and before that at least a month-long break for Onam festival in September. I decided not to go home before the summer vacation and stay back to do some serious studies. Could I live alone in the hostel when all the others went home for holidays? I wondered if Theresa would stay back with me in case she opted not to go home, but I felt that Theresa would certainly go home to meet her boyfriend. It might be better for me to go home and spend a few days with my grandmother and other siblings. I could then walk on my own grounds and Ammalu Athai was sure to serve me with delicious meals. Maybe father and mother would also be happy to have me back and assure themselves that nothing shameful had overtaken me in spite of going to a convent school But did I really want to meet them so soon after leaving home?

What I could not quite understand in my present situation was the hovering presence of God around me. The nuns and their purposeful lives centred around their Divine Spouse seemed to have instilled into me the idea of an unknown zone of which I was quite oblivious so far, but had now become acutely conscious. So long I had been driven by my own needs and instincts, but now, there was some other presence trying to scrutinise me, to make me debate with myself, to slow me down and make me not be so sure as I used to be. Was I on the right path to freedom? I was not used to having any scruples whatsoever when I was at home insisting on whatever I felt, but now I had started questioning myself.

I went to the dormitory to find it deserted since all the others were away. Theresa came back after an hour and tried to engage me in small talk, but I remained unresponsive.

Those were dark days that followed ... I was alone brooding always... the lessons in Chemistry and Physics filled me with notions about a Supreme Power - some kind of a Dynamo behind the universe, manipulating all. Tears and sorrows that oozed out through poems did not seem to matter ... my attention was being riveted to a confluence of abstract powers behind the human scenes. I was afraid that my heart would gradually stop responding to its own beats ... its own needs and prompts.

A dead frog outstretched on a board in the zoology lab... not one, but several of them got ready on separate boards for dissection and study... their limbs stretched and pinned, their bellies slashed, their pear-shaped hearts vibrating rhythmically as the current was passed. It was a ghastly scene, but one from which one had to learn ... our own bodies replicating whatever went on inside those slimy creatures. Sister Patricia was eloquent as she threw light (as well as electric current!) on different parts of the anatomy of the frog and taught us how to dissect and learn. I scored high in practical tests and I could observe even the tiniest of the veins. But I always walked away disgusted with the stench. I had been taught that a human body although similar to that of a frog was different - Man was supreme above all the rest and he was blessed with a hotline to communicate with his Maker. But did one know how to manipulate those wires and make the contact? I was stricken with a sense of inadequacy and felt helpless.

I was leaning against the window looking at the moon. I was seldom in contact with the changing colours of the sky or the growing plants around me after I came to the hostel. There were too many faces to reckon with ... the daily routine was like a ritual to be adhered to, but now I felt aloof from it all and watched the passage of the moon across the sky. Theresa came from behind and laid her hands on my shoulder.

I started visibly.

"Maya," she said, "why are you staring at the moon? Don't you know that the moon's light can make you mad? My mother forbids me even to walk in moonlight. You will lose your reasoning powers and turn into a lunatic. 'Lunar' means that which relates to the moon."

I stared at her almost without comprehension. "How can that be? The sun, the moon, and the stars are ours to watch and derive happiness. What nonsense are you bringing up?"

"Let's go from here, Maya. Let us sit and talk. I will tell you what Sister Agnes told us at the chapel."

"Theresa, I am getting a bit bored with your gossip. I want to be free to think and do whatever I want. Besides, I do not quite like the idea of your clinging to me all the time." Theresa looked baffled and shaken as I said this... she dropped her hands and walked away.

VII

I decided to push forward in my studies and get ahead of the rest. Most of the girls seemed to be bogged down with human frailty and I wanted to be different and superior. I was no longer to be distracted by Theresa and the likes of her, I would not nurture feelings of vulnerability or weakness. When elections were announced for choosing a hostel prefect and floor monitors I was the first to announce my readiness for the post of hostel Prefect. I went up to talk to the hostel warden and started lobbying for myself since I knew that it was not so much the votes, but the warden's approval that was to get me the post. The warden asked me to repeat the Lord's Prayer from memory as a test and drilled me on several rules to keep a close watch on my floor mates. During the study hours I was to make sure that all doors were kept open so that one could check what the girls were doing - were they sleeping or up to some mischief? Before the lights were shut off for the night all doors had to be knocked, the corridors and bathrooms had to be lighted with candles. Then there was the weekly supervision of hygiene and cleanliness in the rooms. During the evening prayer the prefect and monitors stood at the front and led the chant.

All this catered to one's self-worth in terms of others. It gave one a sense of easy access to authorities and it brought recognition. I was happy except during evening prayers ... then, as I led others to examine their conscience, memories of home and pangs of conscience nagged themselves into my mind. Besides, the extra duties of a prefect affected my studies and my progress in the class. The homework was often not quite done and I had to beg for more time. I was no longer free to do whatever I liked. Would I ever be able to discover that new chemical element that Sister Ignatius was always urging us to find?

I tried to lay aside my conscience and all scruples with regard to the past. All these attempts to drill my mind to a set of duties, of rewards and punishments, were proving to be troublesome, creating hurdles in one's path to freedom.

Better to live in the present close to the top, avoiding the scum of regret. I will create an image of myself as successful and free. I avoided meeting with Theresa these days and managed to get myself a room away from the dormitory.

One evening as I was walking around the grounds looking at the plants and flowers and had almost reached the tall boundary walls of the convent, I came face to face with a grotto in the corner that looked almost like a cave with an overhanging black rock. Nestling underneath the rock was a statue of Mother Mary clad in immaculate white holding her radiant child in her arms. Images of flying angels clad in several colours hovered around the Mother and Child, and I stood riveted to the beauty and peace emanating from the scene. Suddenly I became conscious of another figure in front of the grotto -of a tall white-clad nun kneeling rapt in prayer. I felt that I was intruding into an august scene of a solemn reverie and turned back suddenly. The nun opened her eyes and quietly addressed me, "Are you not Maya, the much-talked-about girl in the hostel?"

"I am Maya, but I do not know much about the talk you refer to." The nun got up haltingly and laughed, "What an answer! I have heard about you during conversations in the convent. You are a prefect now, aren't you? And soon after you arrived, you led a protest group to the Principal to complain against the food in the hostel! You are indeed much talked about, my girl!" She was laughing now showing a tiny glimpse of her white teeth.

"May I know who you are, Sister? I have not seen you at all till now."

"Oh! I am Sister Sacramenta. I teach English, but this year I am on leave due to an injury. I fell down in the bathroom and broke my left ankle."

I thought that the Sister was almost laughing at herself as she recounted the way she had fallen and how they had to lift her to a chair before calling the doctor.

"Well, one has to be always careful, my girl! Or one gets into awkward situations."

"Are you okay, now?"

"Yes, more or less. I have come all the way to kneel and pray in front of my Lady."

"Will you start teaching us *next* year?"

"Yes, of course! Besides, you may find me as your hostel warden. Would you like that, my Prefect?"

I could not help smiling at the easy bantering tone she took and walked away with a slight tilt at her ankle. 'This Sister seems to be at peace with herself,' I thought, 'there is no severity or reproach in her words.'

VIII

Should I go back home for the summer vacation? It was going to be an interminable stretch of 60 days and I would have to pack up and get onto a bus to reach my house in the village that was at least 4 hours away. There seemed to be no other alternative since I did not want to look small and helpless in front of the other girls who rushed back home with great expectations. If I were to stay back alone in the hostel I would cut a sorry figure indeed, as I had done during the Onam vacation. Finally however, a circular came saying that all girls were to vacate the rooms during summer vacation and so I had no other option but to go home.

I reached there in the afternoon; I had not announced my arrival in advance. I quietly climbed down from the bus with my luggage and walked home. My brothers and sisters greeted me and my mother urged me to go to the kitchen to eat and refresh myself. My father quietly noted my return. Life at home ran along the same old grooves, meal to meal, sleep to play, play to sleep with several servants to do one's bidding. I was soon ensconced in my old routine and when I remembered my brief sojourn in the convent school I felt a wave of deep excitement and nostalgia as if I had been to a distant land and returned. I eagerly awaited the end of the summer vacation.

The sweltering heat of April and May... long sun-drenched days suffuse with the smell of ripe mangoes, the drone of buzzing flies that hovered around jack fruits split in halves as they hung glued to giant trees. Evenings that brought the rumbling thunder, dark clouds and sudden sprays from the skies at twilight. When children gathered under kerosene lamps, whimpering, tired and hungry, longing to be caressed, fed and led to a world of stories, dreams and sleep, I felt set apart from my siblings and remembered my evening prayers in the convent. Ammalu, as usual, spread out her delectable dishes and insisted on serving me double portions, asking,

"Did those nuns feed you well? How was their cooking? Those Christian cooks that work in those hostels do not know a thing about cleanliness. Have you ever gone into their kitchens? Please Maya, take more of this dish. I have made it specially sweet for you."

The clamour of others and their nagging quarrels did not distract Athai from her special concern for me.

There was now one additional member in that household who awakened my curiosity. A widower nephew of my father had decided to marry again, and a girl had been found for him. This girl, 25 years of age, was one of those so-called 'wall flowers,' born in a very poor family hardly able to provide her with a dowry. Sekhar's nephew, who had lost his wife to a prolonged illness of cancer, was willing to forgo the dowry and marry her in a simple ceremony. I had been absent during this event and now the girl had been brought to the joint family and the couple provided with a room of their own. Usha (that was the girl's name) was very reticent with the members of her newly acquired family and stayed mostly inside her room with the door closed. The servants carried the food for her to her room on a covered plate, and she ate alone.

One day I noticed a kind of commotion around the closed room. The door was bolted from within and a repeated pounding was going on to have it opened. The children gathered around the room and the servants stood here and there, arms akimbo, talking to each other. Finally when the door opened, Usha emerged with her head and face covered and was being led to the gate by none other than her husband. He looked uncharacteristically harsh and was mumbling a volley of words scarcely intelligible. It looked as if he was sending her back to her own house, hardly 5 miles away. The girl seemed unwilling to leave and clung to the doorframe. But Ambi, her husband, pushed her out and came back to the house with decided strides. Almost everyone around seemed to know why this had happened, and when I tried to find out the reason from those who stood gaping, Kunji shot out, "this is what will happen if girls refuse to behave as girls."

My failure to follow family norms and get married had produced a mild flutter of unease among the servants. Even Acharini, our Christian sweeper, and her daughter, Annie, wondered why I had gone to a nun's school instead of getting married. According to the practices of their religion, a girl could choose a vocation as the spouse of the Lord, ('Kartavu', as they said), but why should a scion of a Brahmin family go to a nunnery? But such matters were seldom talked about in the open. Kunji, Velu, Acharini, Annie, Kalluparayan (who brought those finely woven baskets), and Mahmud (who was engaged to climb those coconut trees) inhabited a charmed world of unspoken and contained differences and they retained an unconscious sense of mutual respect for their differences of caste and religion. It was their hard physical toil to earn a living that helped them carry on in the real world.

The holidays were drawing to a close. The annual celebration in the little church up on Kodanad hills was to take place during the last week of my stay. The little village usually left alone by buses and other vehicles now resounded with a non-stop rush of traffic. A sacred cross found there while the workers quarried for stones and bricks had brought instant fame to the neighbourhood and 'the bleeding cross' of Kurusirnudi was visited by hundreds of pilgrims. A retinue of servants from our house did the pilgrimage on foot taking a whole day's leave from work. However, the cook had to stay back to feed the family. I had in the past asked for permission to accompany the servants to the church, but I had not been permitted to do so. This time when a strange silence had crept on the house with all the servants gone for the day, I sat alone and brooded on my school in the convent with its own church. I decided to narrate the story of the bleeding cross at Kurusumudi to the girls in the hostel.

Just a day before my return my father called for me. He was sitting in his large easy chair with his legs up on either side and I noticed that his limbs were visibly shaking as if in excitement. I kept standing in front of him with unease and stared at him. He suddenly shot himself to a sitting posture and addressed me:

"How are your studies going? Are you okay living with those nuns? How much longer are you likely to live there?"

I did not have a ready answer to give him and I kept quiet. "Let me tell you something", he continued, "when you go outside your home you will realise that no one really cares for you. Don't you want someone to take care of you? Don't you want a child of your own to take care of? We have the best system here of arranging everything for your own good... you are already sixteen and in a couple of years you will be too old to get married to a decent family. And what am I going to do with your younger sisters? They are also growing up and it will be difficult to get them married while you block their path like this ... Are you planning to become a nun?"

It now seemed as if the father had turned very persuasive and gentle and was speaking with real concern. His old aggressive authority shattered, he seemed to want to make peace, but on his own terms.

"Let me at least get a degree," I mumbled, "I want to be able to earn my own living."

"But why should you? I am providing for you. And you will have a rich husband."

I remained silent. I did not want to arouse the old sore and he continued,

"You just cannot study to become a doctor or engineer as boys do... do you want to become a clerk or a typist? You don't know how hard it is to survive." He threw away the newspaper he was still holding and got up. That was the end of the meeting. As I turned to go, I found my little brother Balu intently listening outside the door.

IX

So, that was all. My holidays at home were over and I was back in the hostel one evening before the classes started, and as I walked into the hostel, the girls were hurrying to attend the evening prayers. Sister Sacramenta, tall and elegant, dressed in immaculate white greeted them with a radiant smile and as they entered the prayer hall she started them on Lord's Prayer. "Our Father who art in heaven, Thy Will be done on earth as it is in Heaven..."

Yes, the year had started with a new Warden. She seemed to be everywhere smiling and cheering up, spreading a glow of expectation and happiness. I noticed that her ankle had fully healed by now. She did not betray any sign of disability as she walked briskly up and down the stairs. The girls hurried to meet her whenever and wherever she was found. The hostel staff were visibly trying to create a good impression on her. Their lackadaisical ways of serving the girls had clearly undergone a change.

One afternoon, as I had just come back from the class, I met Sister Sacramenta at the entrance. She was talking to one of the staff at the refectory. She was probably remonstrating her on cleanliness and I could hear how gentle and considerate she was even while she disapproved. She then turned around to talk to me:

"Do you want to be elected prefect this year too?"

"I don't know, Sister. I am not doing as well in my studies as I should. Studies are so important to me."

"Of course, they are important. But learning to deal with people and guiding them is even more important."

"I can do it if you think so," I said inconclusively.

Yes, I was selected to be a prefect once again and I looked forward to meeting Sister Sacramenta, our warden, more often. But I could not now pay much attention to my studies or find time to interact with my other teachers. I was now more preoccupied with Sister Sacramenta and my growing admiration for her. I wished to reveal to her all those misgivings that had been troubling me ever since I had arrived at the convent school as a student. A thick pall of gloom settled on me as I brooded and recounted to myself what I would have liked to confide in Sister Sacramenta. I wanted to tell her all about my past, how I had frantically managed to come to that school in the teeth of opposition from the family, how I had rebelled against my parents and been even rejected partially by the family for my disobedience... that I was even now not conscious or repentant of what I had done. I had a yearning to confess, to confide in none but the Sister who it seemed had such boundless understanding, who was ever ready and receptive to the minutest of all problems that troubled her wards. How would she react to and resolve my innermost woes ... my ever nagging pricks of conscience?

"I have aggrieved you by my unworthy conduct," the girls were chanting at the prayer... "I am deeply ashamed and sincerely sorry for having thus offended you..."

"Now Recall," said the evening prayer, "in what way you have acted against the voice of your conscience ..."

The cup of sorrows brewing in my heart seemed to be full at the end of the prayer.

As I sleep-walked out of the hall with a distinct paleness and downcast eyes I was recalled to the presence at the door of Sister Sacramenta with her radiant smile.

I remained withdrawn and unmindful for days afterwards and I could not take any interest in my studies. My mood put off others from addressing me and my teachers found me unresponsive. I was failing in my duties as a student and as a prefect... Others started noticing this change. One day I was called by Sister Sacramenta to her room.

"Whatever is troubling you, my child?"

My eyes were getting clouded. "You don't know what I have been through and how bad I had been, Sister," I burst out, "I am a great sinner. If you know what I really am you will not even talk to me." Sister looked at me closely and laughed with those dancing lights in her eyes. "Not talk to you! I don't think it will ever happen whatever you may have done. Why do you have such dark thoughts?

"Oh, Sister! I don't know how to tell you. I am always thinking ... I am troubled about what I am and what I have done..."

"Please tell me!"

"No! I cannot! Let me go now. I will try later ...". I almost ran to my room and shut the door.

I decided then to set my mind on the terminal exams which were to take place within a month. Soon after the exams they would have a short Onam vacation during which I was expected to go home. I tried to put Sister Sacramenta out of my mind since I could not bear to think of going to her after the last scene I had with her. The Sister also did not also try to follow up our last meeting, but I felt that she now kept an anxious eye on me. She seemed to know my thoughts and she quietly let me go on with my resolve to prepare for the exams.

X

Onam vacation ... once again I was home to face my own people. I felt different this time about home and the people there and I tried to participate in the cheerful festivities of the Onam. There were ten days of celebration to welcome King Mahabali, the legendary King of Kerala who had provoked the Gods to jealousy for the excessive love he got from his people. The Gods had then banished him to the underworld, but had granted him the boon of coming to see his people for ten days in a year. The people rejoiced to welcome him with garlands made with colourful flowers, sumptuous feasts, songs and dances. I enjoyed those days, but it was difficult for me to comprehend why the Gods were so jealous if a man enjoyed himself in the love of his people. Why did the Gods insist on measuring out the happiness for man on their own terms? Wasn't there at least one God with whom one could feel at ease and share one's feelings without the dread of punishment and reward?

Welcome at home was lukewarm as usual and matter of fact. One could tend to the needs of the body and remain mum about the clamour that went on in the mind. My exam grades came by post and my father opened it. The scores were average... nothing spectacular. He summoned me to tell me rather maliciously, "I didn't expect anything better... Good that you have at least passed." I felt subdued and decided to keep quiet and erase all rancour from my mind. I was subdued and depressed for the rest of the holidays and silently watched all the daily activities that went on around me.

Cousin Ambi's wife Usha, who had been sent home rather disgracefully during my last vacation, was now back and I came to know that she was now expecting a baby. She now walked around the rooms with a bulging tummy and seemed to have accepted the house as her own. My little brother Balu had now grown and looked very fat... He often got into tantrums and was severely punished by our father. Our mother had a new baby to tend to ... it was a girl...

a new sister for myself, a puny thing that cried off and on and kept us awake and tense. As my mother reclined on a charpoy on the floor breast-feeding the little thing that sucked so vigorously, Balu lingered around with a scowl on his face and pulled her leg rather harshly ... he sure got himself admonished not at all in gentle terms.

I had two other sisters (not counting the youngest), but I hardly met them these days except during the meals. Of these two, Thankam was several years younger than me and she had just started going to school. She generally kept herself very quiet except when Balu teased her and made her cry. She often ran to our father to complain about Balu, and Sekhar came out looking for Balu to give him a sharp smack. During the lull that had become inevitable due to my studies, plans for the marriage of my sisters were lying low and the relatives anxiously watched Pankaj, closest to me in the line to get married. She had started sprouting buds on her front which caused a general anxiety among them and they advised Saras to provide for a careful cover over her frock. But she was allowed to attend school with an aged escort. The servants once narrated to me with gusto how one day Pankaj had gone and shut herself in the bathroom which had a window opening out to the well. When she did not come out after what seemed a long time, they had knocked on the door with no response. Then they heard something fall into the well and it created an uproar among them. All of them feared that Pankaj had fallen into the well through the window - a desperate act justifiable in her unmarried situation! They had all crowded around the well shouting her name and one of the uncles (it was Ambi according to their report) dragged a long bamboo pole towards the well and tried to push it down the well over the wall. As they were all labouring and sweating in their task and some of them nearly in tears, the bathroom door quietly opened and Pankaj came out after her bath! It was strange that she had not heard any of the commotion she had created ... the splash of bath waters and the loud songs she was singing to herself had kept her totally engrossed! Ambi looked exhausted after the strenuous efforts to rescue her, but he was so happy that nothing had happened to Pankaj.

I often thought of the puny little sister that was still nestling at my mother's breast. What will she do when she grows up like them? Will she face the same kind of problems they had? The mother's milk that she now sucked with such vigour, kicking her limbs, was all that she wanted now. But soon she will start looking for so many other things and then what will happen? That image of my baby sister at peace on her mother's breast took me back to the grotto in the corner of the convent grounds, and memories of Sister Sacramenta came rushing back. What will I tell her when I went back? Could I confide in her all that troubled me?

XI

The rainy season in Kerala had at last come to its tattered end. After the Onam celebrations, people from all walks of life quietly went back to their routine lives. Mahabali, the old king, who had come up from the nether world to make his annual visit to his people had blessed the land and its tillers, and once again, those farmers and workers started ploughing the soaked fields, sowing and planting, and nurturing rosy visions of the abundant harvest in the coming year. I returned to the convent school after the vacation and on the first day of class I had seen my poor grades in the last exam being put up for general view. My mood darkened and I was stricken with self-doubts and remorse at my poor performance. I wandered off alone through the school grounds and found myself standing in front of the grotto. Would I now start praying and entreating the Gods to help me get ahead of all the rest? Or was I just seeking consolation in the Holy Mother as in a mother's lap just like my baby sister at home? Could the gruelling cares of my life so far have a restful focus in a powerful mother quite unlike the real mother I had at home who had simply asked me to obey my father? Where could I find such a real mother to confide in and seek solace? A procession of nightmarish images from the past seemed to rush between my running limbs and I was groping for an anchor to tie myself to in the presence of a gathering storm. The image of Sister Sacramenta, slightly disabled in her ankle, kneeling in front of the grotto haunted me as I stood entranced.

I knew I would not be able to find adequate words to express my present plight. What I had to do was to recast the self image I had of myself all these days and years and tear myself from the fanciful versions of self I had coined for myself. Could I any longer think of myself as being able to be totally free? I felt an urgent need to bend and kneel in front of someone stronger and more powerful to ask for help, consolation, and even some favours. I had not ever felt so helpless, I was not any day so ready to stoop to anyone, not even to my own father and mother. An acute sense of guilt for being less than what I would have liked to be... Free, Blameless and Strong, overwhelmed my will power.

As I returned to my room that evening, I took hold of a pen and paper and began writing down the surging thoughts and images that had kept racking my brain.

"It really breaks my heart," I wrote, "that whatever I write here today will banish me forever from the cherished realm of fond hopes, ideas and illusions I had about myself and my future. I had been driven all these years (not too many years, mind you, only a misdirected fifteen in all) by my ideas and plans of being free not only from all others, but also from God, my creator. It is beyond even my evil heart to keep your holy self in obscurity and misunderstanding about me and my past sins and I cannot allow you to think of me as I am not. Will God (of whom you are so certain and I am not) forgive me if I continue thus ..."

XII

Sacramenta

I found this paper scribbled with black scrawls under my door. It was unsigned, but I could sort of guess who the writer could be. *"That girl, Maya,* "I started thinking as if confronted with a puzzle.

"She had been behaving strangely these days as if she had a ton of bricks on her back and she was too proud to put it down and relax. She has been different from all the rest I have come across under this roof so far. She had been trying to tell me something and getting choked on it. She is too proud and strong-willed and what has she done now! Written a letter and put it under my door! Ha! Ha! what an idea! Taken it straight from the books she reads, I believe. Whatever has happened to her?" I decided to summon her and have a talk with her. But I must never try to rush her... These children ... they need love and assurance before they ever open their mouths.

"Hey! Marykutty! Go and ask Mayakutty to see me!" I shouted to one of my assistants.

Here she comes shy and withdrawn, cringing even to look straight at me... her face looks pinched and her eyes droop... she never does justice to her looks... such ill-fitting clothes and sour expression... how can that girl be released from her cramped self.. how can she be made to reveal all her secret terrors, doubts and scruples and look at this beautiful world and the Supreme Loving presence behind it all ...

"What's all this you have written, Maya, my girl! What's troubling you here? Won't you tell me?"

Maya was cringing even to look at me. Could she bare all her secret terrors, doubts and scruples to this white-clad ethereal figure reaching out as if from another world? Would she be able to express whatever was gnawing at her heart? As I looked at her caressingly with all the concern I felt for her, she began with the most obvious as though she was about to spill a can of beans. "It all amounts to a betrayal of trust under which we live," she began to mumble, "but it has to be said."

"Go on, my dear," I readily responded, "I cannot even dream of you betraying my trust." I made her sit on a chair next to me and took her hand. She pulled her hand away and I could see her eyes filling with tears.

"I am not able to believe in any God, Sister! I have tried and struggled all these days, but God, if at all I think of Him, comes to me only to blame and punish me. He does not grant me any of my wishes, nor does He seem to approve of them. I often think that He either does not care or He is non-existent..."

"What do you wish for, my child?"

"I want to be free, Sister. I want to be able to earn my own living, live in a real world without being always told what I should do and how I should always be grateful and obedient."

"And who is always telling you what you should do? Am I always at your back, my child? Do you find it irksome to follow the rules of the hostel?"

Maya could not control herself any more. A paroxysm of grief overtook her at the thought of being misunderstood ... "Oh! I am not just talking about the hostel," she said. "It was about those days way back at home when I was being forced to give up my wishes to study and be free... forced and driven to conform or be punished as an evil spirit... Ah! Am I not an evil spirit after all... I have indeed done so many acts I should not have, disobeyed my father and my family ... had felt no sense of love or attachment to them. Attachment had only crippled me," she added. "I want only to be left free to pursue whatever I wanted ... I had only wanted to heal and help others and qualify myself to do that... but I was driven to the verge of taking my own life before I somehow managed to get away from it all... but now I feel alone and isolated ... there is a cacophony of voices within my head which would not allow me to concentrate and push myself forward to achieve whatever I had wanted ..."

Maya could not find the words to say any of these clearly and she simply covered her face and wept. As she turned to go away, I held her hand and said, "Don't go away! Tell me whatever you want to. I am not going to punish you or tell you to do anything you don't want to."

Maya looked up at me with eyes glistening with tears, "Sister, is it wrong to want to be different from all the others? Should we always do whatever others are used to? Should girls always marry and serve their husbands?"

I suddenly broke into a peal of laughter as Maya posed her question rather solemnly with a serious face. "Don't you see me here, child, not married like ordinary people, and yet I live a life of service and devotion as I would like to. Don't you think I have managed to be different? We are all different and we can choose our lives differently."

"But that is not what I have been told. In my house we have to do everything as others do. I cannot choose to be different without coming to trouble."

"Well, let us talk about whatever has happened to upset you thus. Why are you so much aggrieved and worried?"

"I cannot believe in any God as you do, Sister. Gods are created by Man in his own image and not vice-versa. I cannot believe in any such."

"You are biting there more than what you know how to chew, my child. Are you not a little fish talking like a whale? Who told you all this? Do you think that my life here devoted to my Lord is only an illusion made up by myself?

"But aren't there so many Gods? They are all supposed to say so many different things. These Gods are used by different people to keep others under control. They hold out threats and punishments in the name of Gods they themselves have created to serve their purpose."

"May God forgive you for saying all these things, Maya. Go and sleep, my child. I will pray for you."

XIII

Maya

'There is always that bit about prayer,' I thought as she moved away. 'They think that prayer can work miracles and fulfill one's wishes. Is it also another illusion created by man for his own convenience?'

A parade of nightmarish voices and images stalked through my uneasy mind as I tried to sleep... praying hands and sinking ships, pictures of erupting volcanoes, flash of lashes, wails and cries, atoms tearing themselves out of all visible objects, bleeding masses, a bleating goat tied to a stump, a blind cow being led to the butcher's shop. In the midst of these scary processions my grandmother appeared quietly taking a cold dip in the village tank, circumambulating the Banyan tree, and praying to Lord Ganesh, that obese sitting figure with the mighty trunk of an elephant. Ammalu too was seen rushing across the bamboo straddle at the gate carrying a sacrificial cock in a bag to be offered to the deities. Oh! In what forms, through what rituals, should one approach a God who was pleased to remain a silent alien presence unless one was ready to give oneself up and grant credence to whatever others said?

Next day I was found hovering around Sister Sacramenta's door. Some other girls were already there and I surmised that they would have a long list of complaints about the food, their roommates and their studies. Then I felt somewhat absurd standing there quite unlike them with my strange fears, with my doubts and complaints about God, and my lack of faith! Then I almost wanted to laugh at myself and belittle my problems. I felt that I was indeed made up of different warring factions within me: I wanted to weep at my plight at the same time I wanted to laugh at myself. Was there a wolf howling within me as I waited there to speak to the much revered nun and seek her blessings.

At last when my turn came to meet the warden, I went up to the Sister and could not suppress a rather shameful smile.

"What is it this time, child?" Sister Sacramenta gave me a radiant smile.

"Oh! nothing special! But, you know you promised to pray for me last time and so I wanted to clear some doubts. To whom do you pray, Sister, and how do you do that? Is it alright for you to pray for only one of your students? Or do you pray in a general way for everyone? Does your God mind if we ask for particular boons? And suppose, a person has done something very wrong, is it still alright to pray to get what she wants?"

The Sister listened to this volley of questions in all seriousness. "What questions do you think of and ask! You can, of course, pray to God, any form of God you are acquainted with, whatever you may have done in the past. In fact, the prayer is a sure way of redeeming yourself from your past mistakes and sins. Don't you know that yet? God's mercy will always forgive you if you confide in Him. That is why we have our evening prayers every day."

"But Sister, if one does not want to mend one's ways even after the prayer ... if one keeps feeling that whatever is done in the past is right ... I am sure God will get to know this ... Is there any point? Would it be honest to pray in such a situation?"

The Sister seemed lost in thought for a moment. Was she going to say that there was no use for prayer if the person does not repent and mend his ways? And which God was she thinking about? Surely it must be Jesus Christ who was said to have accepted punishment for the sins of all the others. Christians believed that Jesus had offered his own life in lieu of those of others who persisted in their sins.

But Sister spoke nothing of Jesus or his religion. She just patted me on my back with gentle affection and pulled me close to her.

"Maya, don't worry about all these troublesome questions. I will pray for you and you can entrust all your worries to me. Have you ever seen a child sleeping peacefully on her mother's breast? I am sure you have, since you have a little sister now, don't you? You should be like that now. You have enough questions to face in your examinations and need not worry about others. You study now and leave all these questions to me."

I was touched to the heart. Here was someone so unlike anyone I had come to know so far. This Sister, or Mother as she wanted to be addressed, was so different from all the members of my own family ... she seemed to enjoy a rare sense of certainty and self-assurance, but still she would not impinge on another's sense of freedom and force her views on any one. She seemed always ready to offer her unconditional support and she left no room for any fears or regrets about whatever had happened in the past. All that I had to do now was to concentrate on the present with my eyes on the future. I felt relieved of my burden of doubts and I went back to my room with a sense of relief as if I had left my future in the hands of someone else.

Yet, I had to admit that what I was now tasting was the pleasure of dependency... I was not striking my own path, but trusting another to help me and promote my cause. My previous sense of defiance and desire to be free and unattached now lay in a heap of confusion and I was exasperated with the changes coming over me.

"Place all your sorrows and troubles on the mother's bosom and sleep peacefully," said a small note that was slipped under my door next morning. Yes, the Sister seemed to repeat, and insist on whatever she had said earlier and it was now up to me to do my part. Would such a condition of faith and dependence apply to all, I wondered. Then no-one needs to struggle so hard to carve out one's own future. One could simply obey one's parents and accept their dictates. I now seemed to understand why most people I had known could live from day to day without a thought for yesterdays and tomorrows. The simple faith that had taken over their minds had become a natural habit for them ... their rituals, ceremonies, and prayers were part of their habitual social behaviour ... they never had to realign themselves to uncertain perspectives, ideas and ways of life... they had a sense of simple faith in the old ways being instilled into them.

But how could one have such a simple faith? I had heard of several arguments and questions and witnessed acts of tearing to shreds whatever another claimed to be true and urgent, the harsh conflict of one will against another when a stronger will always Triumphed. Was God, the Supreme Power that brought such strength and confidence to Sister Sacramenta, such an overwhelming power that one should submit in simple faith without any arguments? But how could such an overwhelming power be also trusted to be gentle and forgiving as Sister made Him out to be? Yes, God after all remained a HE and all those nestling up to Him in submission were expected to behave like women when they married!

The idea did not bring any cheer to my troubled mind ... but as I became tired thinking of my condition as a puzzle hard to resolve, the quiet pleasures of dependency crept on me.. Let Sister take care of it all... All I have to do is to set my mind on my immediate work ... Here was the opportunity granted to me at last by the grace of G-, I did not have to ponder on the clashes of desires, arguments with family, the right and wrong of conduct... I was Free!

Surely then, the fault must have lain in myself as I resisted the traditional ways of life forced upon me ... I had been unnecessarily defiant, I had wantonly rebelled ... I had insisted on having a different way of life. And it had brought on a host of struggles and conflicts... pinches and pricks of conscience, suicidal urges and finally this need to rest and relax on a stranger's lap.

Yes, it was all really confusing in spite of the seeming quiet. Every day during the evening prayer, I, as prefect, read aloud the lines for the Examination of Conscience.

"Now in what way you have acted against the voice of your conscience and disobeyed God, your loving Father. Have you been proud, selfish deceitful?..." The words echoed back to me as the others repeated them. As the session came to its end, I muttered to myself, "No, no, nothing of it for me today. I have only to do my duty and leave the rest with M..."

I kept on receiving miniscule missives of faith under the door ... I did not have to rush to the door of the hostel Warden and heave out my doubts and fears... these messages of encouragement to enable me to continue in simple faith were parcelled out to me every morning. That lovely hymn, 'Lead Kindly Light' written out in a bold beautiful hand, with some leading words underlined (I noticed the double underline on "ONE STEP ENOUGH FOR ME") almost made me search for that guiding light like a toddler lost in the dark. "Knock and it shall Open", were the catchy first words on another day and I wanted to go and knock on Sister's door. Weren't there more walls to scale than doors to open, I later asked myself. "If you have enough faith, my dear, you will be able to fly... to span great distances without having to crawl," said another note.

"Oh! Will I? Will I? I am tired of crawling ... when will I be able to open my eyes and see this glorious world bustling around me," I asked myself.

"Weep with those who weep, Laugh with those who laugh" was another of those thought-provoking messages that sent me rushing to the Sister's door. "What is the meaning of this message?" I asked." Does it mean that I have to lose myself completely in the woes of others?"

"I am speaking of compassion, my child. You should be able to understand others and not criticise them. That is what St. Paul said and it means that you should identify yourself with others."

"Is that what you call love? Is love only compassion? I cannot understand it, Sister. If you can identify yourself with all the girls here and share their feelings would you be able to do any good to anyone in particular?

"Do not raise such questions. Each one gets what is due to him or her. Are you not a student of physics? How come that all those different objects in the world are able to derive whatever they can and need from the rays of the sun? Love or compassion or whatever you may call your sense of connection with others enables you to give and take whatever you need from this glorious world."

"Oh! It is quite hard to understand."

"Do your duty and leave the rest to God." reminded the Sister. "As long as I mediate between you and God praying for your good, you don't have to rack your intrusive intellect. Have simple faith like a child, Maya."

"God has given a new birth to your soul and I am its witness," announced the little missive one day and I felt a surge of excitement. Does it mean that I can now totally erase my past and start all over again? Gradually, day by day I was being acted on by these new ideas of strength and dependence and my mind was opening to new dimensions of feeling. To feel dependent on another, to derive support from a stronger will eager to help no longer seemed as intrusive to my own self will, but the mood was hard to sustain. Like a tyre that is inflated and deflated ever so often, my growing faith in Sister Sacramenta revived and collapsed. I envisioned myself as a young sapling inside which a fluid sap, dark and thick, rose and fell, rose and fell, as I could remember from my lessons in botany. Does God appear only at some intersections which we cross and re-cross, so seldom and infrequently during our long journey, I wondered.

It was that strange four letter word, L 0 V E, that bobbed up and down my consciousness like a piece of cork in a surging sea. No one was free to talk about love in the village I came from, it was a word people were ashamed to pronounce.

(The exact equivalent of LOVE in the local language was indeed a strange word. It was as though that word brought on a feeling that choked at one's throat, brought on a red tinge visible even on a dark complexion ... it made one blush and stop short as if somewhat silly and foolish. I had never heard my father or mother use that word either for each other or for others ... the only time I had heard it in my life at Kupam was when I had eavesdropped in my Hindi teacher's house. Yes, one day the teacher, in between giving lessons had looked troubled, excused himself and rushed to his newly-wed wife in another room sitting and shedding tears. Then I heard those words muttered nervously by the teacher almost in his wife's ear, *"don't doubt my love for you ..."* I had then wondered what he was talking about and why he was so uneasy.

But now Sister Sacramenta often spoke of LOVE ... Not just the love she felt for her wards, but also the love of God that made all things permissible. One could do wrong and seek forgiveness and God loves us enough to forget all our sins, she claimed. Indeed, this made our lives so easy, I thought, it is just some kind of new dependency and one need no longer fear someone more powerful or be harsh on oneself urging to go ahead. Yes, Sister had assured me that everything in life was made easy by just loving, and even the onerous tasks performed with love brought one pleasure and joy. If one is assured of the Love of God one could live a life of joy and peace.

"But how, how, my Sister, how could one get this feeling of love of God and of all the others... what if one is incapable of this feeling?"

"Pray, my child, Pray! If you cannot, I will pray for you. For the present you have only to have faith in me whom you can see. God will reveal Himself to you behind me whenever He wills.

XIV

I had often thought of Sister Ignatius in the midst of all this turmoil with myself and with Sister Sacramenta. Sister Ignatius was the first one to urge me to decide what I should do with my studies... "Discover a new element in Chemistry... Become famous and bring fresh glory to God and your teacher." But how can I do this when I am unable to see anything other than what I was shown? How could I penetrate the veil of the universe and discover a new element? God had indeed built an impenetrable, insurmountable wall in front of everyone!

On the day before the Chemistry examination I sat up late to prepare myself. As I wrote my answers in the examination hall, Sister Ignatius kept on peering into my paper from the back ... I was somehow spewing out those equations and formulae... I wondered at the capacious cavities inside my brain that stocked up everything I had heard in the class.

Those million worlds uncovered in Physics by Miss Susan brought me to different types of imponderable exercise... They set me voyaging on a romantic journey of the universe, but later it cut me down abruptly to a mere speck of dust pulled and pushed around in a whiff in purposeless circumambulation. All the same, the lines had to be drawn straight or curved within the given angles and eyes set on speeding trajectories, thousands of light years away. Those visions of multitudinous particles whirling around in hazy circles around bright flitting nuclei exasperated me. Was God Himself hiding in one of those undiscovered hastening circles of light? Was it His powers of reflection and refraction that was holding us together? The iron grip of the laws of thermodynamics made me seek the consolations of Biology - a simple frog stretched wide on a wooden board with its throbbing heart exposed and swollen. Could I ever become a doctor to tend to the needs of those bodies stretched wide on the rack of this inscrutable universe? Sister Sacramenta continued to teach and recite poetry in her thickly attended classes. Almost tearfully she repeated poems of love and beauties of nature and the human heart written by Wordsworth ... *The Affiiction of Margaret, We are Seven,* and *The Prelude.* "The Sounding cataract haunted me like a Passion," she said, and emphasised the glorious creations of God. When she took up the poems of Keats she dwelt on the endurance of Beauty and Truth. She had an amused sense of tolerance for Shelly's defiance and much-vaunted atheism; like him she hailed the West Wind and demanded its submission. *The Mill on the Floss* by George Eliot was her favourite novel and she expanded on the character traits of Maggie in the book. That little girl clipping away her dark curls in defiance of her aunt's remarks and looking awkward and embarrassed for the rest of the day brought tears of filial love to Sister Sacramenta whose eyes often rested on me gaping in attention from the front bench.

Sister Sacramenta spoke to me in the evening as I aimlessly wandered around the campus after the classes.

"Maya," she said, "I want to give you a book which I would request you to read and keep as a memento from me. Of course, you need not accept all that it says or even read it fully from cover to cover. But just keep it with you as a keepsake from me. Soon you will be going home for the vacation and you can take it with you."

I went up to her to collect the book ... it was nicely wrapped up in a glossy black cover and its first page was beautifully adorned with a painted wreath of flowers and inscribed to me in a lovely hand. The book was titled *Imitation of Christ* by Thomas A Kempis. "Kneel with me here, my child, and write on it in your own hand. Please write, 'I SHALL DO MY DITTY AND LEAVE THE REST TO GOD'. I was overwhelmed by the solemnity of the moment... I took the book in hand to look at the title again and asked in a whisper, "Is this not the same book that Maggie Tulliver was struggling with for years after the loss of all her other books? I remember this title mentioned in George Eliot's novel." The Sister gave me a pleasant smile and patted me on the back for my attentiveness and sharp memory. The book was mine now to browse through and I took it with me when I went home for the vacation.

XV

Home this time seemed quite different. There was a sense of tension in the air and all of them there looked preoccupied and worried. My father kept walking up and down the long veranda and he looked concerned and solicitous as he spoke. Soon I came to know that my grandmother was terminally ill and was lying in her room awaiting her final moment. I put down my suitcase and rushed to my grandmother's corner room.

How many times in the past had I rushed to that room seeking words of consolation and of encouragement! How often had I been comforted and given a share of the old woman's stock of goodies carefully tucked away in a wooden cabinet!

An oil lamp with a faltering wick that had been kept inside lighted in front of a picture of Shiva, Parvati and Ganesh was all the light in that dark room. The grandmother lay cuddled in her bed, but her arms were spread out as if making a final supplication. As I approached nearer, I saw her old frame considerably swollen up, her facial muscles limp and pale, devoid of expression. How could I recognise that dear old soul in that huge, helpless hulk in front of me! The sick woman then opened her eyes ... slits of lights from those dark caverns ... I tried to hold her hands, but her flesh felt rubbery, slipping away from me without any response. My mother appeared behind to call me to the kitchen where Ammalu lounged around in her corner with tearful eyes reciting lines from Ramayana (which she used to sing with the grandmother when they were together early mornings). The house looked as if ready to wail and crack any moment and my brothers and sisters moved around as shadows on pussy feet afraid to ask any questions. My mother shuffled around asking them all to eat and go to sleep.

The lamp at the bedside was kept burning throughout the night. The owls kept hooting and a rain of insects poured into the house from outside, swinging like tipplers kicked out of taverns. I kept my eyes wide open and wanted to sneak into my grandmother's room to have a last word with her. But I knew that Ammalu was guarding the door and would not let me in.

Just before the crack of dawn, just when all those swarm of insects lay collapsed on the floor like a heap of black ash over throbbing globules, a loud wail from the grandmother's room rent the air. All of them got up and ran to her room, but were kept in check by Ammalu and a host of servants. Sekhar took measured steps towards the body of his mother who, enlarged to an unseemly size with dropsy, lay covered with a white cloth.

In the morning a group of professional mourners from the village arrived in the precincts of the house. They expected to be regaled with tea before they could sit around the body and wail for the departed. They started beating their breasts and mourning aloud when Sekhar, who could hear them from his room, came to the scene to stare at those twenty-odd women struggling to heave out their grief through howls and wails. "No need for such histrionics in this house," he said, "I will pay them off" He took out some coins from a corner of the towel he wore around him and counted them carefully before handing them over to Madhav who waited on him. He had already ordered a chosen mango tree to be cut down (was it the same that his father had planted even before he was born?) to be used for cremation in the cemetery. The body was then carried by close relatives who had arrived in large numbers and Sekhar lighted the funeral pyre surrounded by all the male members of his family. He then returned home, shut the door of his room and remained alone for several hours. The women and children crouched together wiping their tears and looking at the empty room left by the grandmother. I sat along with my brothers and sisters as the mysterious pall of death shut out their usual round of activities. I found my thoughts going back to my days in the hostel and the discussions I had with Sister Sacramenta. What would I say to the Sister when I got back? Would the Sister try to console me for the death of a grandmother? Won't she say that it was only God's Will to take away my grandmother? Should we grieve for her by shedding tears and beating on our breast? How do we mourn for our losses in any special way? My father's quiet courage and stoicism had astounded me and I seemed to know he was really grieved. Towards evening, when everyone else was dropping off to sleep, I quietly opened my suitcase and took out the memento given to me by the Sister. I opened the book at random and read out the lines staring at me.

> ***"Thou must be as ready to suffer as to rejoice; thou must be as glad to be poor and needy as to be full and rich. Lord, I will willingly for Thee whatsoever Thou art pleased should befall me. I am willing indifferently to receive from Thy hand good and evil, sweet and bitter, joy and sorrow, and to give Thee thanks for all that happeneth to me."***

I quickly closed the book and a long parade of words and images streamed through my mind. The close resemblance to what I had just read to the lines I used to copy from Bhagawat Gita under my father's orders amazed me. Yes, if one were to accept God's Will, good and evil, sweet and bitter, joy and sorrow could become one and lose their burden of difference, the edge of their conflict and promote infinite joy and peace. The death of my grandmother was an event to be accepted with equanimity just as my father had done.

Next day I found myself walking the same paths around the Ganapathy temple which I was used to as a child holding my grandmother's hands. I circumambulated the Banyan tree and stood rapt in thoughts in front of the elephant God lounging on his stone seat.

XVI

Back to the college at last! The air there seemed to hang heavily with the heat of summer, and a tinge of anxious prescience regarding the final examinations had etched dark shadows on student faces. Everyone was busy mugging up answers from several notebooks and Sister Sacramenta took to walking regularly up and down the long corridor during study hours.

"What will happen to me after these examinations," I wondered. I would get a degree if I passed, but that did not ensure the fulfilment of my plans for the future. I would have to go out to some other institution and seek admission to a professional course if I were to find a job for myself. No-one in my family would encourage or help me to carve out such a future for myself. I waited for an opportunity to discuss the problem with the Sister after the exam. I however quietly studied for the exam without much hue and cry.

The long-awaited meeting with Sister took place when the rest of the girls, jubilant and noisy after the exams, were packing and running up and down bidding farewells to each other. The pressure that had mounted on them during the past few days had suddenly collapsed, the dark clouds that had gathered on the horizon had vanished as in a downpour and the sky seemed bright and clear, beckoning with rosy visions of new adventures.

"I do not know what I will do next," I blurted out timidly. "I know that I must start applying for a professional course and wait for my results. But all my plans seem to go awry and uncertain and I am afflicted with a lack of self-confidence. It was not like this before, I had an excess of self-confidence, but now it is as though I am being dragged through a process of uncertainty and helplessness. Would you say that I have only to pray and keep quiet?"

"If you can not find any help in prayer you just have to give some more time to God. Go home and see what awaits you. Have you ever heard of the expression, **'Letting Go'?** That is what you do now when you quietly cease your frantic efforts and let God do His work. Of course, you must try to find out a suitable course of study and write letters to different institutions. God has blessed you with intelligence and it will all happen at the right time."

I took a tearful leave of my mentor and started packing my cases. The immense burden of my experience, my doubts and fears, faith and hope had taken a toll on my tender years and set me dreaming of sailing on uncertain waters towards an unknown destination. **"Lead,** Kindly Light," I muttered to myself, **"One step enough for me, NOW!"**

* * * * * * * *

AMERICA! AMERICA!

“The United States themselves are essentially the greatest poem”

Walt Whitman

MAYA

I

Why am I so wrapped up in whatever happened in the past and always trying to find words to articulate my experience? Now I am here in America to turn a new leaf of my life and I want to forget my life so far in my ancient country and clutch at that rare sense of freedom I have yearned for. But memories of the past keep haunting me and making me a prisoner although I have struggled so hard to get away from there risking all I have (I do wonder at times what I have left behind... a secure home? a possible husband and children? wealth? power? prestige? land?). But I just sit here brooding over my past and seeking out for words to express myself, but, words crumble in shame or ride past me in disdain even as I try to grasp and possess them. Isn't this all vain seeking, my Lord! Would you not grant me, after the fret and fury of all my blind groping, some rest at least on mere words? Have I now chosen only the seeming stasis of words before an ambitious push for freedom?

I was received at the little airport of the Southern University by Pankaj as was prearranged. She is remotely related to me ... a sort of niece in fact through a cousin of my Chellappa mama. As I came out, I heard her shouting out my name above the airport bustle. She bubbled with energy, grabbed my suitcases and almost ran to the parking lot, dropping a volley of questions on the way.

"How's Chellappa mama? How's Nana? How did you manage to remain unmarried so long? I had heard that you were to be married a long time ago. Did you board from Bombay? ... Ah! Bombay has become a slum these days. I had to hold my nostrils last time I landed there to avoid the stink. Is it better now?" she was rambling on as I sat stunned by the bustling life around me.

The luggage got loaded in the car in the meantime and Pankaj took the wheel. She had not given me a chance to ask her anything and now I said, "So you drive a car here!" But she had already started racing the car in almost a zigzag fashion and my question fell on deaf ears.

I will drop you at the hostel where your accommodation is arranged," she said. "You have to find a roommate willing to live with you if you want to cut the cost." Then with a fractious laugh she continued, "Beware of roommates, my dear! You have to learn to get on with them... you are no longer in India."

I was dropped in front of an apartment building within a complex of many such built in each row with three floors and a wide front. I was ushered into a fair-size room with a kitchen and a bathroom attached, and I was quite taken up with the amenities provided. No roommate yet waiting for me to hone up my skills in human relationships! "Where can I get an air letter to write home?" I ventured to ask Pankaj, "And where is the post box?" "Don't be in a hurry to scribble home", she promptly retorted, "Now you go and find a grocery round the corner to buy some food."

She took the wheel once again and was about to push off when she suddenly stopped with a jerk.

"Don't get too close to the fellows around here," she almost shouted as if to caution me from disaster, "here one cannot just giggle and get away from them as we do back home. They will stop at nothing short of....." she was gone before I grasped the meaning of what she was trying to say.

I sat alone in my apartment and looked at my watch. I had adjusted it to New York time when I had landed at the Land of Liberty and it was showing 3 p.m. Must be at least 2 hours ahead there, I thought *(Oh! It will be dead of night in India now and all of them asleep!}* I sat bolt upright on my lone bed and started brooding on my journey and the purpose of my coming so far away in pursuit of freedom.

I had already spent two nights and a day in New York before setting out for my Southern University. There a friend of my friend, Mr Budhiraj, received me on arrival at J.F.K. airport. He was carrying a placard with my name pinned on to it and it was he who located me before I could set my eyes on that placard. He had an officious air about him and almost immediately after we came out of the airport he told me that he was going to drop me at Tara's apartment before pushing on to Chicago. "Tara would be a better companion for you than me," he said. "You can spend your time with her." As he drove on to Tara's place I remained jet struck and dazzled by those mysterious motorways that crisscrossed and leapt up and down carrying the longest parade of motorcars I had ever seen in my life. "Tara is a very beautiful lady,". Mr Budhiraj whispered. "She wants to be a model, but her husband will not permit her."

"Is she married?" I asked.

"Yes, back home she is married. She is here on a visit to work on a cultural festival". He then leaned closer towards my ear and whispered confidentially, "Don't tell her that I told you. She will be upset with me. She tells everyone here that she is not married ... ha! ha!," and he giggled almost like a teenager imparting secrets. "You have only a day to spend here. Do some sight-seeing and get on well with Tara."

Tara was not at home when we arrived. But no matter, since Budhiraj himself had the key to her apartment. It had the air of being well kept, and a fragrance of flowers ...(or was it an expensive perfume that smelt like flowers?) lingered everywhere. "You can just rest here. She will be back soon. Have a look into that white monster and you may find some Indian curry." He was gone even before I turned to thank him.

Tara arrived at 6 p.m. nearly three hours afterwards. She seemed all excited and in a hurry. The moment she opened the door she called my name and asked me to join her in the car waiting downstairs. "We are going sightseeing. You will like it," she said and I followed her. The waiting car downstairs was nearly full. Several heads with long bedraggled hair turned to look at me and Tara as we approached. They were all male and had impish eyes. "We are all going together," said Tara, "it is Ashok's car. Get in." So I had my hurried glimpses of the great New York city sitting between several young men who talked and laughed incessantly throughout the trip. Mostly they talked of people known only to themselves and of the traffic all around us. Occasionally, I had a bit of their attention thrown at me as to a waiting dog... "this is Manhattan... this is the famous Fifth Avenue ... let us stop here at the Rockefeller Plaza and show her," and so on. At Greenwich village, we did indeed stop 'to look at the gays and hippies' as they put it. They could not conceal from me those sly gleams in their eyes as they looked at the crouching figures on either side of the streets around the Central Square. "These are the kids who protest against their society," someone said with a mild hint of sarcasm. "They are against the

Vietnam war and of every other sign of power and authority. But look! how these males touch and hold each other. They are called gays." Then they all giggled with suppressed mirth. Our interest in those poor creatures remained one-sided, however, since none of those anguish-stricken faces turned to return our looks or nod to us. Tara was watching them closely as if she was trying to draw out from them a special kind of response to her own good looks.

Our sight-seeing in New York was over for the day after we had helped ourselves to slices of Pizza at a wayside shop. As I tried to enter a public urinal, Tara took me aside and spoke in a warning tone, "never, never sit on those seats... the women here suffer from V.D. and one never knows how the infection travels." "What is V.D.?" I asked innocently and got no answer. I was to spend the next day alone at Tara's apartment when Tara went to work, but I was carefully instructed how to use the metro to have a look at the city. The day after, I set out for Wilmington, the seat of my southern university where I was received by Pankaj (as reported earlier.) My stopover in New York had steeled my senses against all public toilets in the U.S. Those lost looks of young Americans in Greenwich village haunted me for a lifetime even as I remembered the disengaged mirth of young Indians who had watched them from a distance. It was only after boarding my plane that I suddenly recalled that I had forgotten to utter even a word of compliment to the exceptional beauty of Tara and her generous hospitality.

II

Now I am at Wilmington sitting on a couch and looking at my watch once again. Pankaj had been gone a long time and I realise that I have to set myself going and find the things I need to eat and study in the campus. I decide to take a walk and look around. Oh! How interesting it is indeed to walk around the campus! Not many are around at this time since the school is yet to reopen for the Fall session. For the first time I noticed the bright blue American sky shining on me and I breathed the clear robust air that sent a wave of thrill through my body. I saw those trees on which the leaves, some of them at least, had turned pale and yellow and were nodding their heads to me in friendly welcome. Amidst those multiple colours of green, yellow and red, tall trees of pine and oak stood their ground and acted as sentinels to gathering darkness. A rich peel of church bells suddenly vibrated through the still air and my heart pulsated with sheer joy. Oh! To be alive in such a pleasant place with those sweet soothing sounds to take off all the cares! I remembered home only to brush away all thoughts of what I had left behind there to be rewarded with the sight of this vast panorama beckoning me to a delightful ecstasy.

"You are from Bombay, did you say? You must meet this lady Mrs McMohan who is so interested in Indian students," the Foreign Students Advisor told me next day as I visited his office. "She has been to the sub-continent several times and gives a party every now and then to the foreign students. Her husband is a well known doctor and she has registered for doctoral work in International Relations. Would you like to go to a party next Friday? I can arrange to pick you up from the hostel."

"Yes, of course."

I gratefully accepted the offer since it was something to look forward to at the weekend. Meanwhile, all the formalities of my registration completed,

I had taken my assigned place in the English Deptartment with a chair and table at the corner of a large hall where many other graduates had their seats assigned. I was the only one from India and I received friendly attention.

There were at least 50 foreign students at Mrs McMohan's Friday party. Some of them were new to America and to such parties and they stood in small groups while others, used to such occasions, moved from one to another introducing themselves and starting a conversation. The lady herself was surrounded by a group of her guests and she welcomed them, chatting incessantly. She was very much at ease with everyone and she had a friendly word or two for each one as she moved sprightly through the room. "I was in Bombay last week," she told me, "I like that city. It has life." I was delighted to hear those words about the place I had come from, which had only recently been maligned by my own relative, Pankaj. I felt very grateful to Mrs McMohan. Just then someone was tearing her way through the crowd to talk to me. As I looked up I saw Pankaj all decked up in beautiful clothes and jewellery and trying to grab my hand.

"I did not know you were coming here," she said. "I could have picked you up. Have you settled down? Have you found someone to move with you?"

"Yes, I am looking for someone from our Department."

"I think you should look for an Indian roommate," Pankaj muttered. "American girls indulge in a lot of nocturnal activities. Don't be daft." She had a way of speaking that reminded me of some people back home who assumed an instant authority over others and came out with uncalled for 'no-nonsense' comments. Pankaj took me back home from the party. That nice lady, Mrs McMohan, a friend of India and Indians, came to have a chat with us before we left and encouraged me to get in touch with her if I ever needed anything. I felt quite at home in America while she was with me and started thinking that India and America were not so far from each other. With such emissaries of understanding between the two countries, will not all differences vanish? Pankaj again rudely broke into my reverie as we were driving home.

"Let me tell you what happened at McMohan's two years back," she said turning to me while she was still holding the wheel, "Linda had brought an Arab student to her house and she invited him to stay there for a couple of days. She kept herself busy looking after his comforts, cooking meals and fixing his bed and so on. Then one night, when her husband was out, the Arab invited her to his bed! Ha.. ha ..."

"And then?"

"I don't know what then... she must have slept with him ... or thrown him out... there are two versions of this rumour. I believe the first... or else why should she carry on like this ..." Pankaj was once again rapping me on the wrist even as I was trying to crawl. Why should she bring such sexual innuendos in her conversation? Should sex and sexual fantasies enter into all such encounters with her? As I sat still in the car half listening to her, my memories rushed to my own past experiences back home in the village:

(A vociferous group of people had assembled around her, my friend, Mala. She was lying on the floor, a spectacle of abject misery and howling with acute pain. I had just gone there to meet her and I was taken aback in utter confusion. Mala, my dearest friend ... how have you come to this...? her incessant desperate sobs had sent shivers through my spine and I stood there numb with grief. The group around her were her own family members ... her father who had always greeted me, her uncle who looked grave and forbidding, her cousins and aunts whom I hardly spoke to. Now they had all surrounded Mala's crouching body and I suddenly noticed they were smearing her eyes with a green paste. She screamed every time they approached her and they shouted abuses at her. "Shameless slut! Shameless slut that has brought such dishonour to our family. You think you can get away with this? Tie up her hands! Let us see how far she will go. We will tear him to pieces ... Don't we know where to hit him, tear him to pieces, and break him to pieces?" Someone hit Mala on her back and pulled her hands. They tried to break into that cordon of grief, children screamed and women sobbed as the guardians of morality advanced with chilli paste in their hands).

When Pankaj arrived at the door of my hostel she had to shake me out of my dark reverie. I had indeed gone into a daze floating in the memories from the past.

III

I walked around the campus next day watching various sights. The way different people dressed themselves provoked my curiosity and amusement. There was not much that could be called a dress in some cases - a matter of gaps and absences in places where one expected to find a cover. The parts of those bodies thus exposed were gorgeous to look at, fair, well-nourished and well-shaped with visible energy in active motion. I suddenly became conscious that I was there encased in this piece of saree cloth from neck to toe and I wondered whether I could ever set my body to such exposure and free movements.

The informality of classrooms amazes me... Dr Healy, one of my teachers walks around the class room, taps our desks every now and then and goes on with the lessons. At times, he goes and sits in a chair petting his beard and seems to be in deep thought. There were more interrogatives in his lectures than statements; of course there were no imperatives at all in whatever he said. He expects us to answer every question he raises even in the middle of his sentences. At times I feel he is making faces at us and asking us to make our own facial responses in return. It is indeed a lesson in body language involving an active engagement in ideas and their expression ... no passive gulping down or pushing down the throat.

"How are novels written?" he thunders, "have you ever thought about it from the writer's point of view? Eking out those volley of words to enumerate the events of the days, months and years, to express one's experiences... Is that it? Did I hear someone say 'not by any chance' to my question? Let me intervene, friends, Who wants to spend one's time just nibbling at another's experiences? What do we do with feelings? Convert them to words? Do we want a transcript of another's mental history? What for? How do we, the readers, benefit from such exposures? Take the case of our famous writer, Ernest Hemingway ... Have you heard of him over there?"

He seemed to address this question to me, but I kept mum. "That great machismo of a writer was good at hunting and at f...ing; he got a great deal of kicks from watching bullfights and was a great lover of women. But finally he put a bullet through his head... what do we get out of his books? His message and his code? Have you ever thought of that?"

Dr Healy went on with his lecture and the class kept quiet. The boy sitting next to me unwrapped a gum and put it in his mouth. The chewing went on unperturbed by the rising pitch of Dr Healy's voice. A girl in front of me took out a cucumber from her bag, chopped it vertically with a table knife she produced from nowhere, and salted its sides with a cute little salt shaker she picked up casually from inside her bag. She could now be seen holding the wedges and taking an occasional snipe at them as she listened to the Professor. No one other than me gave her as much as an interested glance. As I watched her with rapt attention I had slipped into a trance from my own past:

(She had smelt her palm again and again ... A pleasant odour of green mangoes and jasmine was coming from the middle of her right palm ... She could hardly resist smelling it again and again ... that overripe smell of fruit, flower and flesh. AYYA Sar was hammering on his algebra lessons then and she had lost touch with his loud voice. He sat on a high creaky chair with a cane in his hand and rolled his luminous eyes at everyone. Suddenly he had turned to ask her, "if 'a' equals 2 + 3 and 'b' equals 4 - 1 what is (a + b) x (a - b)?" She stood up with her palm on her nose and fumbled for an answer. The frail man afire with the mysteries of algebra took hold of the cane and cracked her on the palm again and again. "That is for not listening," he said, "for doing your own things while the class is going on." She bore the lashes stoically and when she again unconsciously raised her palm to her nose, the whole class burst into laughter).

I woke up from my reverie to listen to Prof. Healy once again as he was pounding the desk and going on in his lecture:

"What of Hemingway who wrote of codes and courage, but finally in a desperate moment put a bullet through his head? Words ... words ... words ... we honour them only for their words... They can give us only words and passing passionate moments." Professor Healy was coming to the end of the day's lesson and distributing a long reading list.

Next day, as I walked along the corridor, I had to pass by Professor Healy's office room. I looked at him across the open doorway. He was inhaling from a long pipe, but I could not see even a small wisp of smoke anywhere. His eyes seemed screwed into his face just above the squat nose, and patches of grey wiry hair seemed planted onto his terracotta head. He was all agog with courtesy and good manners as I stopped at his door ... Obviously he expected questions. "Sir, does a writer have to be a great man? If a man cannot live with his own truth is he eligible to write for others?"

I asked him this question out of the blue; I did not know that it was coming. He took the pipe out of his mouth and held it rather stylishly between his fingers. I noticed a wart on his second finger top left. I looked for a wisp of smoke from the open end of the pipe ...

"It all depends," he said, "what do you think? Doesn't one experience truth through words? Have you read Hemingway's books? How many have you read?" He started sucking from his pipe with a dismissive gesture.

It was a general sense of lack of idealism that puzzled me in my first observation of an American classroom. The centre seemed to have fallen out... 'do as you like' attitude... more questions than *answers*... no role models ... no heroes ... Back home *we* were used to worshipping so many.

IV

I had met Mrs Brown at Mrs McMohan's party. She was one of those charming local women I had been introduced to and she had warmly welcomed me. I was pleasantly surprised one day to meet her again at the edge of her own garden which happened to extend to the street by which I walked to school. She recognised me and invited me into the house which looked very cute with a large sitting room and a brightly lit porch. "We like India and the Indians," Mrs Brown said, "and we waylay them as they walk to school." She had a nice set of pearly teeth and her smile gave out a genuine sense of cheer. "How are you, my dear? We met at McMohan's and I have never found you on this street. How are your studies?"

I planted myself firmly on her couch and she continued, "We are Mennonites. Strangers are welcome to our house. Our great grandfather left his homeland to come to this country as a stranger, and see, now we can take care of strangers in our house. Praised be the Lord!" She was a believer. She had a family coat of arms made up of her own high self-esteem and Christian humility. "If you like I can take you to our church on a Sunday morning. We have a new speaker and you can meet an interesting group of people."

"I will be delighted," I said and remembered my own stay in a convent college for several years.

(Oh! my Sister Sacramental You had prayed and prayed for me in that church attached to the nunnery and assured me of God's protection.)

Just then, a young girl walked into the room carrying a load of books which she carelessly threw across the room. "Meet Judy, my eldest daughter," said Mrs Brown. I turned to look at her with extended hands, but she declined to shake hands responding only with a casual 'Hi'. She seemed reticent with her cold blue eyes, but I wanted to carry on a conversation with her. She was a student in the university and I wished to know more about her studies and other interests as a student. While she remained withdrawn and quiet, her mother proceeded to give me some information about Judy's preoccupations.

"She is a leader of Students' Movement against the Vietnam War," Mrs. Brown said, "and she has just come after giving a speech on the podium. You know how politically conscious students are these days. Judy takes active interest in whatever goes on in the campus and she participates in marches and demonstrations. But she also takes courses and is bent on graduating next year." I could see that Mrs.Brown was proud of her daughter.

(yes, That was how it was in America! I thought, parents encouraged their children to participate in politics! Can I forget what happened to me in India when I wanted to join the Freedom movement?)

"No! No!" he had shouted at her... "none of this Gandhi business in our family. No mixing with waifs, strays and vagabonds and walking round the dirty streets holding flags! They will drag you everywhere, you have to urinate on the roads, they will rape you and put you in a jail along with thieves. Is that what you want? I have arranged this respectable marriage for you. I have even paid for it in hard cash and you want to run around in the muck with hooligans. The British did for India whatever the Indians never could ... they gave people like me an education, a rational approach and creature comforts. What more do we want? What can these satyagrahis give you, you rebellious idiot?" He pulled her by the arm and made her sit cross-legged in the middle of the room. Her little brothers and sisters, and a whole bunch of servants and onlookers watched her humiliation. "Go on repeating 'Narayana! Narayana!' one thousand and one times! If that does not tame your disobedient heart write down the first ten slokas of Bhagawat Gita, Chapter 12 at least 500 times." He threw the book at her and walked away. Afterwards, as a mark of protest she had stopped wearing her bangles and gold chain. She had refused to comb her hair and when the bridegroom's parents arrived to settle the marriage she wanted to be seen with a dismal face without a single ounce of gold on her. She even planned to send her gold chain and bangles secretly to Gandhiji to help him in his struggle against the British. But that was not to be.... The groom's parents never arrived ... they had heard those village rumours about the girl who had behaved most inappropriately in a respectable family. And whatever happened to her as a result ... those horrible days of

seething agony, moments of terror and punishment that tore at the very fabric of her dreams and turned them to nightmares...

"Would you like to go to the church with me this Sunday morning?" Mrs Brown was asking me when I looked up from my flow of memories down under.

"Yes, yes, the church is it? I am familiar with it during my studies in the convent college. Although I was not a Christian by birth I know all about the church and prayers."

There were many eager faces at the church door on that Sunday morning. "Knock and It Shall be Open," "Seek and Ye Shall Find," were boldly written on the wall bringing me nostalgic memories of Sister Sacramenta. There was a rosy tint of expectation in all those waiting and seeking eyes and as I struggled with the onrush of my own memories, Mrs Brown ushered me into the midst of that jolly company and I tried to pull myself back to the present scene. The new Speaker of the day, Rev. Francis Thompson, had just announced his subject. He was going to speak on 'Why I Have Become a Christian.'

The speech was lyrically charged with intense emotions, but it was also self-congratulatory and assertive. Every now and then a chorus of voices from the crowd arose in unison and punctuated his speech: "Oh, hear him, o my Lord, hear him, and bless us." At the end, as the speaker sat down exhausted, his golden cup of thick red persuasive passion overflowing on to others, they all rose together and moved towards the alter to pay their homage.

"Tea and Refreshments will be served in the next room," someone announced over the loud speaker. Mrs Brown held my hands and pulled me towards the front. "Have you any questions to ask our speaker?" she asked me with great interest.

It was Good Friday. I knew that my Sister will be attending the Mass in the chapel and will come to the hostel only late in the day. It was raining heavily and I felt sad and gloomy. "One has to make great sacrifices for God's pleasure," she had told me on the previous night, "So learn to suffer. Only suffering can purify your soul. Renounce your earthly pleasures and pray for God's mercy. That is your only salvation, my child"

"Do you also suffer, my Sister?" I had asked her.

"What else is my life for, other than suffering? But I enjoy my suffering because it is only to please God"

Here in America they seem to rejoice in God, and not suffer. Am I right? Will God become more friendly and helpful to me now since I am in America?

Mrs Brown offered me some cookies and a cup of coffee. I was invited to lunch in her house.

V

I sat late into the night reading books. The night was still and calm, the deep blue sky of daytime lost in darkness. I thought of home and all that I had experienced there in my home and in the convent ... The words in the book in front of me floated on white pale pages and took strange turns and formed curious combinations. They acted like little chess men playing by themselves without a player ... the king and the queen looked daggers at each other, the horse took some funny jumps, the bishops stared and the little pawns giggled like mischievous imps and sneaked around. I shook myself to look steadily at the page and reinstalled those naughty miscreants on their proper places. But soon, I stood up and started pacing up and down. The wooden floor of the room resounded with strange thuds as I walked and I mistook them for the loud beats of my own heart. Echoes of wild laughter floated in from a neighbouring house. There were burning lights and a clamorous company. It seemed to be a wild get together ... they roared with laughter and sang snatches of popular songs.

I wonder whether one ever forgets. We carry all we have experienced wherever we go, however far we travel... it all comes back like a rising tide and hits the edges of one's waking hours ... My father ... his laughter too had that wild glint of mirth, it did not blend with the rest of him that was so stiff and implacable. Why do we think that laughter always wells up from joy? Could it not be just a kind of bodily spasm that spurts and releases whatever one has within?

Next day early morning. I made fresh resolutions to leave the past alone and keep living only in the present... classes, library, assignments, the incessant search and struggles for the right words on blank spaces.

I was called to Professor Blake's office to discuss my term paper on Research Methodology and collect my grade. I had submitted the paper nearly a week ago and he took the paper from his file to hand it back to me.

"Sit down," he said, and went on wryly, "I notice that you have no sense at all of right punctuation. Comas, semi colons, colons, full stops and all such other signs should hold your paper together, but they do not make any proper sense in your paper. You use too many dashes and they reveal the frequent breaks in your thoughts. Go through my markings on your paper and see what you can make of them."

As I opened the clipped sheets of my paper, a curled 'C' stared back at me from the front page and the following sheets were all dotted with red marks. Curlicues, circles and underlines were littered on them as though a jet of red ink had been casually sprayed on them in an attempt to produce an occult design.

It was indeed appalling ... my own panic and vulnerability. Or else why should I now run to Professor Healy with those sheets stamped with marks of my own shameful performance? Nervously I entered his room and showed him those papers, and said that I could not understand whatever was wrong with my sentences... my manner of binding them and breaking them. He glanced at those sheets and muttered, "Ah, those punctuation marks! The foreign students are always weak in tackling those. You have to learn the natural rhythms of speech and think of the meanings you want to convey."

He then proceeded carefully to prepare a pack of note cards with lavish illustrations of the use of comas, semicolons, colons in a number of well thought-out sentences and underlined the key junctures with red and blue pencils. I felt he was giving me a gift when he handed those cards to me (I have preserved them to this day) and felt extremely grateful. I sat up till late at night to study those note cards and absorb those signs of meaningful communication into my thinking. I felt helpless: all tied up in knots when my thoughts broke out like a rushing torrent, wild, untamed like some rivers in India that need to be dammed with cunning designs, nuts, bolts and mortar. I turned and tossed in my disturbed dreams with those note cards strewn all over me.

The door bell was ringing like a long wail. Someone was knocking on the door. I had to gather myself and open my eyes before I could go to the door. It was Pankaj standing at the door and she had a wild light in her eyes. "Come in, Pankaj. So early in the morning." I turned to close the door and found that she had already seated herself on my open bed.

"I can't stand it, I can't stand it any more." She cried out, "Everyday! everyday it goes on in the next room. She, my roommate, never comes home before 2 a.m. and then she brings him with her. His boots on the stairs wake me up and I know they are there. The wooden floor creaks as they turn and toss, and then there are all those whispers and mutters. And then they open the tap, and the flow of water is like a loud report. How can anyone have a peaceful night? Oh, I can't carry on like this anymore... we are here to study and make for ourselves a bright future, and we have to witness such activities every night. One cannot be an onlooker and go on as if nothing happens." She stopped and looked around my room.

"You live alone, don't you? Haven't found a roommate yet?" she asked as I proceeded to the kitchen to make some tea. "Let me stay with you, Maya, for some days and then I can find something else. But my notice period ... I will have to forgo my deposit."

It was from that day onwards that Pankaj started staying with me. I had not yet learnt to say 'no' to anyone and assert my own preferences and so I fell in line with her request.

She began sharing with me lots of snatches and snippets of news from around the campus. She pounced on the vagaries of behaviour she came across in people and gave me a graphic account. One Chakrapani, for example, an elderly business man from South India who had turned a student in his late years was making himself ridiculous with his eating habits! He brought with him a mixture of rice and curds with a heap of red pickle and ate it with his hands in front of everyone! He had a dark portly frame which some Indians considered disgraceful and he did not have a shred of good manners. He often cleared his throat and spat out too loudly. He often sat facing the wall away from people and tried to create his own private space when people talked around him. Pankaj also reported on people who came on student visas and started raising a family without an iota of shame! One Mr Singh has had three children while he was engaged in writing his Ph.D. thesis! His wife had no other work, she kept house, cooked and raised the children. And then when he had to have a sudden appendicitis operation he simply passed a hat around in his Department, in the church and among those he knew! They did help him, of course, that is one thing good about these Americans ... when one is down under and asks for help, they help for sure. Dr McMohan, our friend's husband did not even charge the operation fees!

VI

I was spending more time at the library these days to finish my assignments. As I walked back late at night with my head swaying with information and ideas I had gathered from books, I entered an aura of unreality. My own experiences back home in India, the memories of my parents who tried in vain to get me married and my own vain attempts to understand my country... its ways of hurting and healing its own people receded to the rear end of my mental baggage to assume distorted and unfamiliar shapes. Books had now become more real to me than my own life that had shrunken to the size of the crumpled face of a clock.

I measured the tides of human passion by what happened within the passages of novels I was assigned to read. Back home, the world of books had no sense of reality or relevance for me, but now books alone seem to measure out my sense of reality of life. I walked like my own shadow nowadays and tried to reckon with the images within a kaleidoscope guarded by sable-clad figures. The blonde hair and fair faces of my neighbours in the library became part of my dream world and my head swam with the ideas and characters from the pages of books. I felt strange sensations and vibrations travelling up and down my body and I heard certain door knobs turn within my head and felt the presence of someone cleaning up the house, bringing the cobwebs down in heaps and twisted shapes. There was the sound of dusting, knocking, and swabbing ... My eyes winked at sudden lights, the harsh sound of footsteps strained my eardrums ... I am like one intoxicated. What after all is real and what is unreal... my own name... a phantom to my faded sense of reality, ceased to make any difference. Whatever was far away became real, and the unreal took hold of me as I surrendered to let myself float down a fairy stream. Do I dare to ask whence ...? why ...? what for?

I have become a thing apart from myself I rarely talk to even Pankaj these days. She lies snoring mildly, twisted to form a 'v' or 's' or curled into a coma as I get ready in the morning to go to the library and again, she is either tossing up and down or starkly absent when I get back. When some people on my way smiled or greeted me I look at them through a film in my eyes. It is 'Good Morning' to 'Good Morning' ... 'it's cold' for 'it's cold,' 'hai' for 'hai'... a dreamy monotonous ritual of repetition that sounded remote even to my own ears.

Today as I went up the stairs I saw Professor Healy coming down in a thoughtful mood. He had in fact come very close to me before I recognised him, and my sudden sense of his presence broke through my veil of unreality. Even before I knew what I was doing, I had flashed a smile at him and greeted him in an unconscious surge of joy. He must have been baffled by my response, I am sure, and when by chance I met him again on the stairs he looked oddly at me and I withdrew my eyes. I remembered his eyes and stark stare several times during the course of that day. It was as if a real being with eyes, face, muscles, limbs and all had strayed into my world of books. He mingled with the other fictional characters in my mind and achieved a sense of overwhelming presence. He seemed to know them all and he could, with a mere look of his eyes, command them to submission. I trembled at this on-going drama within myself and longed to shield myself, to take cover and return to the placidity of my bookish world. I went home early that day and looked forward to hearing all that gossip which Pankaj had gathered to narrate to me whenever she got a chance.

Pankaj was waiting for me as I entered my room. She had a troubled look. "Is there any evil rumour that is going round to put you in such ill humour?" I asked trying to put on a light tone. But she sulked and waited for me to express some concern. "What is it, Pankaj? Are you back early today?"

In her sitting pose she stooped to ward off my searching eyes. "I never thought that it would happen to me," she murmured almost inaudibly.

"What has happened?"

"Oh, only whatever happens to everyone here... But this time it is me. And I can't understand it."

"Tell me what it is and who it is," I insisted.

Words came slowly, chokingly, almost inaudibly from Pankaj. "I come from a conservative Brahmin family," Pankaj began, "and my parents allowed me to come here so that I may go back with a degree and some money. But now, this boy here has stolen my heart and claims my whole being."

"Who is it?"

"An American... tall and very fair." She suddenly sat up with stars coming back to her eyes.

"But why are you in such an ill humour for that? You should be happy."

"But my parents, my mama, and all the others... what will they say? You see I never thought that I could love an American, but now, I am drawn without my knowing why ... Am I wrong?"

A shrill call from the phone startled both of us and I let her take the call. I could sense a sudden change in her mood ... she kept talking for a long time with exclamations of ecstasy, longing and submission.

The days were getting shorter. The beautiful autumn days replete with colours, resplendent in golden light turned to grey and my heart trembled with unknown terrors. As I moved about the campus I could barely make out people's faces draped in caps and woollens, and reflecting the rays of artificial lights switched on early in the evening to keep off the thickening darkness of winter nights. Seminar talks, term papers, and final exams proved to be the staple of an otherwise dreary fare offered to the students in the midst of darkening shadows and we walked around briskly in pursuit of these beckoning goals.

I met Prof. Healy once again against those artificial lights one evening and I trembled when he greeted me with those casual words, 'it's cold.'

I wished I could say something very bright in reply, but what I said was a mere nothing - a belated 'how are you?' Those eyes followed me all the way to my room and stared at me from the pages of my book.

News from India was being published on the top pages of newspapers and projected on to T.V. screens. Usually we rarely come across Indian news in American papers and we keep our curiosity switched off to escape from our troubling sense of intrusive loyalties. But now the news headlines hit us everywhere. India's war with Pakistan recharged us with an intense sense of patriotism, and our nostalgia for our homes, our people and the warmth of national togetherness made us numb with grief. There were some meetings and speeches in the campus, but many of us tried to keep quiet and let the adverse comments go past us unquestioned. Ramunna, now settled on a dreary government job in Bombay, wrote to me about the bomb scares in Bombay when the whole city was asked to switch off all the lights in the evenings. Policemen were going round with torches to enforce the rules and my blood coursed through my veins trembling with unknown fears streaked with guilt.

"Oh my country! mymotherland! Ancient land of glory! Why am I thrown into such quandaries and conflicts to end up as a quaking mass of exhausted nerves in spite of the struggles I had to face in my country to seek my freedom in a foreign land!"

"Don't we take too moral a stand on all issues everywhere?" Pankaj asked me suddenly one evening. She was living in her own world these days ... our paths seldom crossed, but I could see that she was too preoccupied with her own affairs to mind her obligations in living with me. I wanted to let her know that it was time for her move out. Although she never brought her friend home during late hours, I could sense his presence in the room during my absence. The clean and crisp tidiness of my room was broken through with unwelcome signs of intrusion... the sink stacked up with dishes, large footprints in the bathroom, sudden appearance of stains and crinkles on the couch covers. Then one day, a single wavy blonde hair in the wash basin had thrown me nearly into a fit and I had decided to have it out with Pankaj before long ... and now this question from Pankaj staring me in the face in the midst of a war that our country, the country of both of us, was engaged in. "Don't we take too moral a stand?"

She was asking me, and I sharply retorted, "What exactly do you mean by that, Pankaj?" There was a challenging note in my tone and she at once was duly submissive.

"I mean about our relation with other countries ... say for example, Pakistan. Couldn't we have done better with a less moral stand and more understanding?"

"I am not quite sure what you are talking about," I said. "If you mean people, we should always show understanding, but if you talk of countries, there is only national interest. Foreign policies are not just moral weapons."

I knew that Pankaj was only trying to draw me into a conversation and thaw the ice that had been forming between us. She was also being brainwashed by her American boyfriend, I told myself. So I mumbled something about having to meet someone and left the room. I wanted to talk to her seriously when she was less loquacious and more repentant.

I think I have now reached an impasse... Words fail to stay within my grasp... they slip away like errant boys. I have to struggle with them, slap them to do my bidding, but they mimic and parody my efforts and I feel embarrassed. Better I leave them alone and let them leave me alone. Facts and fiction intersect, cross and re-cross within the interstices of my brain and they part in haste to go their separate ways.

VII

"The American writer has always had to face the problem of finding his own language." Professor Thorpe was haranguing the class. "Our forefathers came to this country with their Elizabethan English and they were followed by several waves of non-English speaking immigrants. The land was new and names had to be given. Language was something to be appropriated, not merely borrowed. Take the case of Hawthorne, Eliot and Faulkner ..."

I felt a sense of dismay at this revelation about finding one's own language. Haven't the Americans spoken English for centuries? Why should they stumble at handling it? They had possessive rights over their language unlike we, poor Indians, groping for the right word and the right sentence, and always being distracted by a thousand random echoes and intrusions from various other tongues including one's own mother tongue. ***'What are we? My God! Does an Indian in his own land possess a language of his own?*** I was to remember this lecture of Professor Thorpe for a long time and it disturbs me as I have no other option but to write in English and keep these records of my American experience. I remember my recent struggles with comas, semicolons, colons and other meaningful signs in language and I am afraid of making intrusions into what is not my own. And are these the reasons for my nervous twitches as I make my efforts at articulation, my sudden sense of '**tongue-tiedness?'**

I had to walk all across the corridor or else I have to take the stairs to the left. But I was already walking across the corridor and right in the middle of it to the left was his room. It was open and a flood of sunlight poured across the door to light up an enchanted spot in front of me. As I stepped into the light I turned my head to the left. He was just lighting his pipe and he looked up. I greeted him and stopped looking at my watch. I had started feeling uneasy. "How are you doing with your studies? Are you all right?" he asked.

"Yes, yes, but I feel very cold here." I blurted out.

"Are you homesick? If I were you I wouldn't have stirred out so far leaving my own people," he said.

My tongue seemed to be stuck to my throat as I tried to say, "I had so many problems there. I wanted to find answers for them in America and then return," but I could not say it. I felt a slight shiver and I kept looking entranced at his pipe. I could now see a whiff of smoke. "Why are you so uneasy when you come here?" he asked. Again I tried to grasp at words and felt embarrassed. "I have to go to class," I said as I turned to leave the room.

When I returned home that evening, I knew that Pankaj had decided to move out. She would have told me that much earlier if I had found time to talk to her. Now I knew that she was going when I saw her packing.

No scenes, no harsh words ... she left thanking me. I was sure that I was going to miss her.

Oh, my God! Let me put this in here itself... that huge ache in my heart about Pankaj. Nearly a month after she left I heard my phone ring, and someone told me that Pankaj had met with an accident on the road The guy was driving and they were on their way north somewhere... it was a fatal collision ... I couldn't believe it. The images of Pankaj telling me her various stories, her coming to the airport to receive me and her retreat into herself after she met this boy... my mind was choked and I sat holding the receiver in my hands. Later, after a couple of days I was called to the mortuary to identify her body. I heard myself squealing and closing my eyes as I saw her body tightly wrapped, but her face, Oh, God! Restless even in death terrifying with scars and stitches. I wrote a letter to her mama the same night full of praises for her.

VIII

The winter finally arrived. For the first time in my life I could see the snowflakes coming down in zigzags of white rushing ribbons from a brooding grey sky. I was thrilled to see them coming to rest for a second on the sleeves of my big red coat and dissolve into a moist patch, and as the sky opened to shower more and more snow they settled on me, my hair, my coat, my eyes... I felt a strange excitement coursing through my veins. *'This is snow... This is real snow,'* I kept muttering, *the snow on the Himalayas which we yearn in vain to see and touch has now actually come to me.'* My excitement acted as an antidote to the chill brought by the snow and I trotted back to the hostel carrying all that snow with me. I saw some others opening out their umbrellas as if this extraordinary experience could be meted out the same treatment as an ordinary rain!

Christmas time ... those sweet peals from the church ushered us to an enchanted world ... the insistent notes of the piano playing 'Auld Lang Syne'... The golden sunlight that mellowed the familiar campus walks ... my God! Such beauty and peace...can it really exist? ... Exist for me who is only a mere stranger here crammed with more questions than I can ever hope to find answers for... a troubled soul with an unstable past... and an uncertain future.

DO YOUR DUTY AND LEAVE THE REST TO GOD... She had taken my hand holding the pen and made me write on that blank space on the book she called her 'memento'.

"I am giving you a new birth today. You shall live a peaceful life from now onwards. All that you have to do is to do your Duty and leave the rest to God," she said.

My hand trembled as she held it firmly and I wrote the words. The pattern of black and white scrawls on that tiny page gripped my ***mind***

and tightened its hold on me like a chain. The rest was supposed to be all smooth and easy ... one has only to do one's duty and leave the rest to God. I had walked away as if a trial was over... But not before she had kissed me and blessed me after making me kneel with her.

Yes... a troubled soul... That was me in those days with a barrage of doubts and questions to throw at everyone... why, why, why ... Why study? Why follow the rules? What's love and what's ego? Why do parents in the name of love assert their will over the children? Why does one become a nun? Do the nuns really renounce all? What's the meaning of life? And what of GOD, GODS and Prayer? A host of such questions from me had once troubled me as well as my mentor and guide... a nun herself. She had tried to quiet down my unrest for days to come ... she had initiated me to a world of duty, love and trust with a chain of black and white words on a book and a kiss on my forehead!

Christmas Eve was spent at Mrs. Brown's house. That sweet cherub-like face, all aglow and busy, running back and forth from the kitchen while Mr. Brown relaxed on the sofa talking to foreign students invited for the occasion. Judy in a sober plaid dress, her hair nicely combed and knotted, seemed cheerful and content. I carried a gift to the family; so did other foreign students. We all sat and chatted, and Judy came and sat next to me. She told me that she was going out with an Indian boy ...

No, he was not present there at the moment... he had gone elsewhere... but he would be in for the New Year.

This boy, she said, belonged to an ancient Indian family and he was studying to be an engineer. "But he would then go back to India and serve his country...

"I too would go with him and help the people," Judy added. "He belongs to Uttar Pradesh," Judy continued, "lots of farmers there and his family owns a lot of land. They were even called maharajas at one time."

Her misplaced accents amused me, but I did not try to correct her. "Are you planning to marry him?" I ventured to ask. "Well, maybe," came the answer.

Those marriages in India... Can Judy commit herself to one of those and live there helping people? I wondered about what she told me as I tossed in my lonely bed after the party. Why couldn't I do whatever Judy planned to do and stay on in India instead of coming here to find my freedom and answers to my questions**? 'Do your duty and leave the rest to God...' What is my duty? What was my duty?**

As the grey winter morning light peeped through my window blinds I lay there on my crumpled sheets with no clear light to show me my path to duty. I then relapsed into a trance that brought me those nightmarish images of marriages in India.

They said there back home that the rains came to relieve the Earth from the agony over unmarried daughters. When it came as it did often in the afternoon before a wedding day it augured well. But the work had to be done, dripping wet or holding palm leaves over the heads or carrying umbrellas that rose like balloons in the howling winds. Servants ran about the house and around the newly erected 'pandal'. They carried baskets of vegetables, large-sized brass vessels and several bags of provisions needed by the cooks who had just arrived and sat around rolling tobacco and snuff or exchanging gossip with one another. The cleaners walked through the scene timidly with large brooms, mop cloth and cleaning buckets, some of them tried to drain and wipe the dripping water that formed patches on the floor. As soon as the twilight settled and the rain went away, at least four petromax lamps were brought in by a group of local boys and they engaged themselves in pumping the pistons as if to coax and wheedle the genie that held those bright lights captive inside those rusty frames. And then at last, the lights poured out and enveloped the whole house and illuminated the decorated pandal. No bride could sleep that night ... she only lay quietly as though asleep even as she kept hearing all those household sounds around her. The bright gas lights from the busy kitchen swayed every now and then to send their wavering beams across the dark corridors to other parts of the house where prostrate figures lay huddled in hallways and twitched their muscles as the sounds and lights came floating down to awaken their muffled senses. Busy loud-mouthed people clustered like moths around those lights hanging from crude contraptions carelessly attached to the old ceiling. Even children who should have been in bed at such late hours had their eyes wide open for those bright lights and the delicious smells of savouries that came from the kitchen. They challenged each other in nervous whispers to go near the lamps and swing them to and fro ... and then suddenly the sharp voice of an adult barked at them, "you rascals! Do you want to kill yourselves? Don't go near those lights! Go to your beds at once!"

Such were the images that floated through my mind regarding those wedding days I had watched from a distance and shunned away in my own aspirations for freedom. Did I also not know whatever those brides had to go through after such luminous weddings? Did women ever have their own dreams fulfilled after their weddings? Were they able to have any plan at all in their tender age? What will happen to Judy after her marriage to an Indian in Uttar Pradesh? She will have a really colourful wedding but what will happen to all her plans after the wedding?

Suddenly I was woken up by a loud bark as I was floating in my dream and I sat up rubbing my eyes. No! No! it was not true! No marriage was being arranged for me... I was still in America, the LAND OF MY DREAMS FOR FREEDOM...

Yes, those sleepless nights before every family wedding ... eyes closed, but sounds and smells always pouring in... loud echoing laughter ... shuffle of feet, the creaking of dragged vessels, the loud report of coconut shells being broken, the smell of hot oil and boiling syrup. Here in far away America, lost and cut off from all my people, I was only engaged in a shadow fight with the past, and my mind tried to close itself like petals at sundown ... Memories of distant past flitted by again, time had not consumed them; they roamed around the dark corners of the mind.

'I *wept after every one of my childbirths,"* I heard a distinct voice in my nightmare,

"I mean, every time except when my Raja was born. But he came last after I had given birth to five girls in a row. That is my fate." She was in tears as she said this and lifted the corner of her saree to wipe her eyes. But Savitri, the woman from the house down the road who was always ready to lend a helping hand, had quickly cut her short and said, "Paru, you have everything you need, you have land, money and gold. Why do you moan for your daughters? They are fair (unlike the father's side of their family), and clever; they have no physical defects. Why do you grieve for them? Just think of my sister who has six daughters ... she cannot muster enough dowry for even two of them. How will she find anyone to marry them?" Paru stopped short of tears and she seemed to review her position. But she could not help saying, "Just think of the botheration and work I have to do ... If I had only

boys I would be escorted as a chief guest to my boy's marriage and I will order everyone to do my bidding. But I have to go through the marriage of five girls before my Raja gets married. Tomorrow we have to feed hundreds including all the waifs and strays of the village. That is what it means to celebrate a girl's wedding. The bridegroom's party, more than forty strong will arrive as real lords of the event and we have to do their bidding." "Don't worry", Savitri consoled her, "we are here to help you ... Let us go and see how the ladus have turned out... They should be kept away from ants and flies. We will see to the 'kolam' and flowers afterwards." Several local women, all set to help in the festivities had gathered in the room. They did not mind sitting in the dark on thin charpoys and they were engaged in subdued whispers not to disturb others who wanted to catch a wink or two of sleep. "But just think of this girl Maya who refuses to marry," one of them said "Do you know that even the rains refuse to come down to wash the earth when the girls refuse to marry?"

I stayed in my bed the whole morning seething and struggling with my nightmares; my memories bounced back and forth from the past to the present like coiled springs. My father, the landlord of the village who had three daughters and two sons, had made me the target of his fury because I had refused to marry as every girl did; he had chased me around the house with a stick... I was only twelve, but I had the wrong kind of ideas for a girl and had to be tamed and turned into a true member of the family.

"Don't you want some silk sarees to go with those? Nice silk sarees are available in Coimbatore and the next time your mama goes there we will get you half a dozen," my mother had announced.

"Where will I go wearing them? I don't need them to go to school," I said.

"School? Are you going to school forever? It is time to stop school, Maya. Do you know that you have grown?"

She looked at the rising buds on my breasts which were pushing and holding up the pink flowers printed on my gown. "Father has decided," she said summarily and moved on to the kitchen. I had then ran to my grandmother, my single ally in the whole house, who alone could dare to ask my father to change his mind once it was made up. But as that old woman sat there in her corner room munching molasses and flat rice she looked helpless; she only told me how important it was for a girl to get married and obey her father.

"Come, try a bit of this," she said holding out a piece of 'gud' that leaked through her fingers.

"I will have none of that", I had replied curtly as I walked to the door. That was how it had started... my defiance and my disobedience ... the constant carping, coaxing and threatening, no more going to school and the constant bickering, "You look so grown up, cover your breast with a saree, you can't wear frocks or skirts any more... Go to the kitchen ... learn to cook ... don't sit on the veranda ... don't spread your legs ... don't speak to me... have you no shame to disobey your father? Get married and learn to get what you want from your husband... see how that cow licks its calf... don't you want a child of your own to love and kiss ...? If you stay here any longer you have to work as our cook..."

Oh! All those derisive looks and comments on one's body and to its ever-swelling parts ... its first streak of blood and five days of seclusion... Sleepless nights of tossing on bare floors... vast stretches of emptiness ... life's potion turned sour... bitter potion creeping up and down to the limbs.

IX

On this Christmas Day in America, lost in an Efficiency Apartment in a Woman's Hostel, those nightmares from my past have now overwhelmed my senses. I raise my head from the pillow to look at the time on my watch. I struggle past the bed to dial Mrs Brown and wish her a happy Christmas. She is still in bed after last night's party and is annoyed that it is I on the phone so soon after the party last night.

Nothing much to do on a holiday like this except wash, cook, eat and sleep. The anticipatory delights of Christmas day already over, only the routine work remains to be done...it is vacation time. The classes won't start until after *two* weeks.

I was fully awake and up very early in the morning ... I could hear the birds jabbering up the snow-covered branches. There were faint streaks of light on patches of white that spread like a shroud over the gaping holes of the windows. I was trying to get up and go out into the stirring life of another day. What untold tales of joy or agony might lie concealed within the jabbering sounds of creatures all around in the early morning hours!

I had heard once such muffled whispers on an early morning like this when the rest of the house lay asleep. I had tossed away my bed sheets to walk outside and hear those birds singing on mango trees. But I stopped dead and listened to those whispers ... whispers that took on a manly vigour and choked some feeble protests. Man and woman, father and mother, lying together in the next room, whispering, talking and moving to and fro.

"If she is my daughter she will do what I say... I will break her if she carries on like this ... what am I to do with so many children, you and your daughters! Am I not man? Are these mine or not?"

My mother, poor thing, trying to appease him, to flatter his manliness, whispering back in feeble begging tones, "she will no doubt do whatever you say ... she is only a child ...but soon she will come down crawling"... Oh! That was enough to make one feel a stranger in one's own house at a tender age... to lose one's sense of identity and belonging ... to accept the fact that one has to coddle, fear and surrender ...

The pressure had mounted from that day onwards ... It was like living in a condemned cell under constant threat and scrutiny ...the only way to escape was to get married ... that means that one will be reabsorbed into the system... to the luxury of gold bangles, chains, sarees, and, of course, to tender flesh of babies and to a man's body, its incursions and righteous claims.

DO YOUR DUTY AND LEAVE THE REST TO GOD... These words had been stamped for ever into the very fibre of her being as a result of those struggles and attempts to get away from them. That label came with her as part of her baggage to America from the nun's school ... happily, of course, and trustingly, but naively perhaps ...

I could not even say the word LOVE in those days... it stuck in my throat and pulled down my tongue... it made me look pink and awkward ... it had something to do with the flesh I hated and felt apologetic about, it resembled the long red dripping tongue of cows licking the gummy, hairy back of new-born calves, the roguish eyes of bulls turning to hazy red as they wagged their stiff tails trying to caress and mount the backs of she-animals with throaty, husky moos and hoarse breathings ... Such were the images that came to me with those four letters ...

L 0 V E... but inside the dark interiors of that nun's school 'Love' seemed to take on fairy wings and beckon to an ethereal world from which the bodies had vanished. The nuns spoke frequently of love and it brought a glow to their eyes which I wanted to shrink from, but could not. God's Love was all embracing, they said again and again, and called upon us to respond to it in a similar fashion.

In America, almost everyone spoke of love and frequently fell into it. Take Judy, for example, she had fallen in love with an Indian and would go to Uttar Pradesh to live and work with him! Can I ever imagine doing such a thing?

I remembered Pankaj and her ill-fated love affair and shuddered almost involuntarily.

The village had seethed with rumours and wild stories when I left for the convent school. The girl was mad, someone said; she had a lover abroad, another said; she was kept in chains and so she wanted to run away, yet another confirmed. No one was really sure what it was all about except that a family name of good standing was being dragged in the mire by the mere slip of a girl... a bad seed from its own loins... a sad instance of a bud not nipped in time and growing into a demon tree.

X

I got up and looked around my window. The snow had started falling and those trees on the pathway were thickly covered with snow forming eerie snowy designs against a patchy sky. Not a trace of green anywhere around, leaves and branches all gone, and all that was left was snow, white and pure pouring from the skies... a gift of the angels or a shroud of death...? It was a supreme sight, a moment of revelation ...

What if one grossly failed even after doing one's duty? Aren't there too many duties - a host of them in fact - beckoning one to different directions at once? When one leaves all the rest to God to sort it all out, one has also to learn to accept failure, a failure, maybe, only in the world's sense, but nevertheless a failure that all can see.

Wouldn't it be really a disgrace to get all those Bs and Cs on one's grade sheet when the classes resumed after Christmas? The joy would go out of everything and one had to live with a diminished self-image. I kept spending more time with books in the library than with the few people I knew. Home-sickness lay like a pall over my senses and I realised that there were no short cuts to achieve good results. One should keep on working and leave the rest to God. Ideas and images from the past haunted me and kept dancing with the words in the book. I kick start myself and screw up my eyes on the page, but my own fears, anxieties and experiences, past and present, have become part of the parade of words and sentences in front of me. What have I gained so far from books and teachers in spite of my nagging pursuit of them? All those struggles in my childhood and the bitter fights at home were all done in the name of books and study and they have remained to haunt me even at the advent of my new life in the new world ...

It was the day to worship Goddess Saraswathi, the Goddess of learning. Sekhar, the landlord and her father, did not care much for rituals and festivals. Reason and Use were the names he gave to his Gods... 'Man has to create his own Gods,' he said, 'to meet his own needs.' But Saras was different... so were the rest of the household, relatives, servants and hangers-on. Saras liked the expectant air of ceremonial occasions, the servants being ordered to wash and clean, to collect the flowers and heap them on bright freshly polished 'thambalam'... The children stripped of night clothes and given a bath in cold gurgling water tiptoed around, the vadyar arrived wearing a wet white loincloth to squat in front of a freshly made kolam and clang the bells for all to hear. Clad in a fresh saree, with her wet hair tied behind her back, Saras would ask him almost obsequiously, 'do you need ghee? Do you need camphor? Shall I dispatch Velu to the pond across the road to pluck the lotus flowers that grow midstream?' and so on. The priest would sit unabashed by such anxious queries... his lips would move in tandem as he lisped those mantras... What one could hear from those whispering movements every now and then was 'Bhagavane Krishna, Bhagavane Krishna: a frantic call to Lord Krishna for his blessings. As the Puja started with the lighting of a lamp and the centre fire, the bells would boldly clang and the children would be asked to bring their books to be worshipped and sprayed with holy water ... Maya lay twisted double and wept on that day... her books, the books she had when she was still in school were to be fetched for the Puja, but she had refused since she was no longer allowed to attend school. Ever since the marriage proposal came and she had refused to marry, all those bitter fights and tears, all the twisting of arms and lashing of whips had followed and she had been torn away from schools and learning. She had just collapsed on the bed and started weeping inconsolably that morning and failed to appear at the Puja; she could offer the Goddess only her tears as an offering. But soon she was dragged out of her corner, and a tirade of abuses followed, "You, mudhevi, (harbinger of bad luck), you are like a widow lying in a corner on this festival day, you, who has said 'no' to your own wedding blessedness... is that how you welcome the Goddess to our house?" Maya had only looked away and wept ... her facial muscles twisted and trembled like birches in a storm, tears had poured out and a deep yell lay muffled to choke her throat... Oh! Goddess, are we here only to do what others lay on us? Can I not be given what I want directly by you?

Yes, learning had indeed been fun in the school... the moments of thrill and adventure into the unknown realms of numbers, words, pictures and patterns. The teachers were held in high esteem within the premises of the school although they slid down in people's eyes outside the school where they were often found brooding in the midst of a large family of several children and dolled-up wives, not to speak of widowed aunts and cousins. There was, for example, Nanu Sar dressed in a loincloth, his long hair tied up in a knot behind his receding front line, thrusting a different view of him from the front... he seemed to be two different persons from the back and front... his sober pinched face and eyes glistened with heaped-up knowledge in the front, but he had luxurious curls and a large black mole at the back. He seemed to like having crawling kids all over him as he lay flat on a wide swinging plank at the front room of his small house... (That swinging plank was indeed a delight to climb on... one could push it standing on the floor and then try to climb on it as it moved ... it was like trying to climb on a moving bus ... it was often a hit and miss attempt full of thrills which turned to unspeakable ecstasy when one managed to climb on to some part of the teacher's voluminous body as it reclined and swung with the plank ... it was one's first contact with a man's body.. its odd assortment of damp hair all over... long sinewy arms, the abrupt mound of a nose that revealed a cavernous depth, glittering flame like eyes that suddenly opened and closed and that strange moving thing underneath his loincloth ...) At school, of course, Nanu Sar was an upright man, he drilled those lessons right into one's head and chained them to the shifting sands of one's perennial memories. He always had a well cut switch right on the table which he used without flinching whenever any of the children erred, dawdled or let out unwanted sounds.

Now one sat in the midst of books checked into one's carrel in the cold depths of the Central Library. There were also others who also sat in their carrels screwed to their seats and ignored the world around. They were pussy-footed when they moved around (which they seldom did considering all the reading they had to do). But whenever we came face to face, which was rare, they sure emitted those *hellos, mornings* and *howdys* that brought a warm tide sweep through one's blood ... Learning, learning from numerous books and all their cross references and cross comments seeped through one in a strange land ... But it was nothing like my schooling in that remote village where the body and the body language, aspirations and dreams commingled to form the hard core of one's yearnings about all the things one did not know and wanted to possess.

XI

Margie sat right next to my carrel. She had blue eyes and blonde hair and the warmth of her sudden smiles was hard to resist. I felt very friendly towards her since she had many memories of India to share with me. Her parents had been missionaries in India when she was a child and she had many stories of ayahs and elephants as well as of her journeys across a continent full of unknown dangers, thrills, strange customs and manners. I liked to listen to her although my own childhood in my country was so different from whatever she depicted and narrated with nostalgia using such unfamiliar images.

Together we went one day to have a swim - it was Margie's idea. It was a dark cold day and the chill air froze the blood, "Don't worry. It is a heated pool," Margie said. The pool looked inviting, filled with blue waters with a silver sheen at the top. Clad in a bright green bikini Margie looked like a water-sprite and she leaped upon the silvery glass to break it into tiny shards making room for her to glide forward.

"Come on," she said resting on her arms and gently moving her feet.

"I am ready," I said as I held my nose and made an awkward pose to take a plunge. "I swim slowly. I cannot keep pace with you."

"Let me see, let me see, let me diagnose your problem ..." I landed with a thud on the shallow waters.

"You barely manage to float," Margie said, "but why do you bend your knees? You don't seem to use your legs at all in swimming ... what a pity! I swim mostly only with my legs. That is what gives me force."

"Do I not use my legs?" I asked, "I can feel them. I can feel their weight and their cumbrous movement."

"But that is no way to use them ... stretch them out as far as they can go and move from side to side... No, don't do it up and down ... you would only drown yourself that way. Keep to the surface, keep to the breadth and never to the depth. There is an inhibition at the knee. Get it over with ... stretch, stretch, side to side."

"I get so tired ... look, I am breathless. I will have to go to the side and hold the rim," I said as I rested for a while. Holding the projecting corner of the granite I tried to move my legs from side to side without a grip at the knee. It was hard to get over that grip... it clutched like a vice. Yet when I could free myself even for a few seconds I heaved a sigh of relief; it was as though a silent insistent twitch of pain between the muscles at the back was suddenly lifted ... as if a coil of spring long compressed within the dark dungeon of a barrel was suddenly released to jump into the bright thin air without.

That was the beginning of my swimming lessons in America. In the remote Indian village where I grew up they tied me to one end of a long saree and threw me casually into the middle of a pond to swim back if I could; if I couldn't, they simply pulled me back with the other end of the cloth ... there it was a mere struggle for survival, but here one had to be conscious of the different parts of the body ... that twitch at the knee, for example.

"Am I doing it all right now?" I asked Margie next time we went to the pool.

"Let me see... you still plunge deep into the water ... Not necessary, not necessary at all. You get tired because you go so deep. Then, my dear, why do you paddle like a dog with those hands of yours? Throw them forward and take a bold leap."

"Oh! I am so confused ... The hands are the only things that help me float alive... please leave them alone."

"That way you can never swim fast without tiring. Dog paddling won't do for a good swimmer. There! You are trying to cover too much ground with your hands. Bring them closer ... Throw them back ... if you let them go out too wide you cannot get any force in throwing back."

I realised that there were many things I had to do together to be effective. If I concentrated on the movement of my feet, I forgot my hands, and if I started to train my hands, my feet were lost and out of control. "I cannot synchronize; did you hear that? I just cannot synchronize! That is what is wrong with me! What shall I do now? I am tired," I shouted.

"Don't worry ... we will stop for the day ... these are just the basics. There are several other tricks I can show you ... Maybe next time." Margie said in a soothing tone.

The pool was already empty when we looked around. Others must have watched the clock and finished their swim on time. They had left a trail of water drops, drips from the edges of their costumes. Those who walked behind the first ones trampled on the earlier marks making them look like impressions of giant feet placed one upon another. I felt an empty sense of fatigue at the core of my being as if I had been sucked out of vital fluids that had made me tick all these years. I knew that I could not survive in America only on my instincts and I shrank from using all my faculties at the same time.

XII

New Year Eve... the year 1971 was round the corner. An Indian couple invited me to join them in the New Year festivities. "You have to dance," they said. "I do not know how to," I replied apologetically. While in India I had once visited an elegant club where those social ladies moved to the rhythm of waltz and foxtrot, but I was scared out of my wits at the prospect of such unknown movements.

"Don't worry," said my hostess, Mrs.Singh, "here you will see another type of dance. They don't follow the rules here any more, you could just shake your hips, trot about and call yourself a dancer. You should not miss such a grand sight."

So I agreed to join them and the three of us arrived at the venue around 10 p.m. eager to greet the next year. Mr. and Mrs. Singh carried with them a bag full of goodies and snacks as well as several bottles of cold beer. It was a dark night lit by remote stars, and the air was chill outside although inside the hall as we entered, the crush of people gave out a peculiar warmth. They sat around in groups under an ill-lit canopy and they chatted and clapped boisterously to the rhythm of loud music. Almost everyone had a glass in front of them and they indulged themselves in fun and jokes as if they did not have a care in the world. The music wailed loudly like battle horns prior to the start of a battle.

Fat white bucks in a wine-barrel room
Barrel house kings, with feet unstable
Sagged and reeled and pounded on the table
Pounded on the table
Beat an empty barrel with the handle of a broom
BOOM BOOM BOOM

The dark lit hall was full of moving shadows - shadows that seemed to come to life in their vigorous movements and loud responses to one another. I kept watching them from the safety of a corner seat while my Indian friends melted into the crowd of dancing white bodies in the room. The flowing garment of Mrs. Singh flashed bright colours into the scene and I was swept off by my memories of the music lessons my mother had tried to arrange for me in preparation for my marriage. I also thought of Indian festivals and dances which I had watched at random. Music and dance were considered part of the rituals of life in India whereas here it seemed to be sheer fun. I sat there watching all those who were moving so unselfconsciously, some of them with huge sagging bodies pulling themselves together and trying to imitate the gaiety of general commotion with their ridiculous steps. One pulled the other too close, hampering free movement; many sealed their lips with those of their partners seeking a state of silent ecstasy. Darkness emboldened them, the strange bodies that one rubbed against in darkness seemed to acquire a blissful warmth, a distinct glow of desire floated into the eyes as the music reached its highest pitch before coming to a sudden halt. There was a mad rush back towards the tables, bottles were opened with popping whiz as the aspiring froth came to fill up sparkling glasses. With the next stroke of the drum there was an increased tempo in the movements all around. The heads now kept on swinging with the feet, the hands clutched tighter, the bellies sagged and the glints in the eyes became more pronounced. Darkness deepened and one could now see only dark shadows lost in a volley of fantastic motion. Clutching each other as if to keep steady and not to fall, they were like the human likeness of shadows made to move by mechanical means. I wondered whether a man I was staring at was not almost twisting and distorting the soft female arms that clung to him so helplessly. The most awaited event came when the midnight stroke was heard; there was a scrambling of wild unsteady feet, people fell on one another swept away in an unknown sense of blind excitement, they no longer cared whom they kissed since the wet humanity of another's lips was all they sought to feel. There was no longer any sense of colour, dress or nation, they flew to one another and hugged each other with a sense of causeless brotherhood. One tottering old man caught me unawares in his flight of passion and planted a kiss on my shocked lips... he moved on to his next target as I squirmed under his foul breath and wiped my lips.

The revels were ended as the night advanced. Leaning figures crowded on doorways searching for car keys in their bags and pockets. Their hands shook as they searched and they took note of the drizzling rain outside. The one who managed to find their keys and cars stopped at the porch to pick up their friends and one could see how the chill downpour had steadied their faces and given them a new look of caution. I waited in front of a door quaking within my shoes and watched the cars advancing and disappearing with a flash of their bright lights on the dark wet driveways. I noticed that we had left behind huge heaps of bottles, numerous stray bottle-tops, half-emptied cups with stale liquor, and also unseen dust of several indistinguishable feet to rub against the expectations of the new -born year.

I had another invitation soon after and that was from Mrs. Brown to attend a group-singing by handicapped girls from an institution. It was a charity performance and Mrs. Brown was delighted to participate in such events. She had an exalted sense of life and its ideals and she was not always happy with what went on by the name of entertainment in the usual television channels. She would rather attend an event where those poor girls tried to sing and release their pent-up feelings, and give her a chance to make some contribution to their betterment. So there she was on a Friday night in an unusually happy frame of mind, her pretty brown hair arranged in shining curls and wearing a charming blue frock. One little tingle of her horn near my door and I was out like an eager bride all dressed up for the occasion. The function was arranged in a small hall brightly lit and there were many waiting already exchanging mutual greetings. A group of singers made their appearance on the dais. They were young and tender with dreaming eyes open with an abstract gaze. They gathered together like birds flying towards a common nest and stood still as if for a signal after making a deep obeisance. The signal given, they melted into strains of melody slightly lifting up their chins in a statuesque pose. The song lingered in the air; they seemed to have poured out their soul into their songs that reverberated back to give them new life. Mrs. Brown gently turned towards me and whispered, "It is the first time they make their appearance. They have just come out of the hospital." The audience responded with a hearty applause.

It was raining when we came out. It was chill and dark, and the cars splashed thick jets of muddy water. I shook within my coat and clung to the vast body of Mrs Brown and shuddered when we came to my door and I had to take leave of the cosy warmth of her breath to plunge into the chill darkness outside. The gloomy windows of my lonely apartment held out a revolting look and I knew that I was going to be very unhappy during the night. I remembered that I had woken up that morning with a sense of gladness. I now repeated to myself the old Indian proverb that said "if you wake up laughing you shall sleep weeping, if you wake up weeping, you shall laugh when you go to bed." Does Nature have such ruthless rules?

XIII

The day broke loud and clear and I stretched myself in front of the mirror. There was a ray of sunlight breaking through the window pane leaving a solitary bright spot on the dark muddy floor and it revealed innumerable specs of dark dust circling around. The sky was a blue canopy and the bare branches of trees formed incomprehensible patterns pointing towards the sky. The wind prowled around shaking all susceptible objects and it pounded on the body entering the blood stream through the clean pores of the skin. As people stepped outside their doors they felt the slight tremor of chill and pulled their coats to stuff their hands in the pockets. I looked at a tiny bit of lonely cloud shaped like a little boat floating wearily across the sky swept by a strong tide. Suddenly it stopped overhead and cast its shadow on the passers by.

An old man was sitting on his door steps and watching the passers on the road. I had seen him sitting there almost every day with a bent frame and rheumy eyes. He always managed to mutter a 'howdy' when people passed by him and seemed very agreeable to continue the conversation. One evening, I had seen him digging a small hole in his garden as his frame shook a little, but his hands clutched at his tool with easy mastery. I had greeted him and started a conversation about the changing weather, and now, everyday as I passed by, we met as old friends. As I walked towards my office, Mr Griffiths, an assistant of the Department, was seen sitting in front of a pile of cards in different colours. He always looked up when he heard footsteps and started an easy informal talk.

"Hello! We have to do a lot of useless work in our country. It kills my soul to answer all these piles of correspondence and keep record of all the floating mass of information that keep pouring on my desk every hour. Do they work like this in your country?"

"In my country!" I exclaimed, "People there also complain about their work and they are generally months behind due dates. But there is not so much pressure from the top there. They all take it easy, chat and keep complaining. It is difficult to get a job in India, but once you have it you can relax."

"I wish we could do it here too," he replied, "but we never can. Our soul gets a chill if we go home without completing our work and sit down to watch the TV shows. What religion do you follow, may I ask?"

"I am a Hindu, a high caste Brahmin," I said emphasising on the word 'caste' to get his reaction.

"Do you still have your caste system in India?" he could barely conceal the mild tinge of superiority every citizen in an egalitarian society like America felt towards countries that still kept the caste system.

"No! We no longer accept it! Our Constitution forbids it. The western ideals of culture are penetrating so deeply these days that caste is no longer a practical fact. We too believe in democracy!"

"The largest democracy of the world, isn't it? But how long will it take you to feed all the individual mouths?"

"I don't know. Maybe as long as it takes to reap a big harvest," I said trying to move away before Mr Griffith could ply me with another question with regard to Indian harvests.

But he called after me this time with a request, "Could you please get for me some lines from Bhagawat Gita in Sanskrit script with translation in English? I would like to put it up on the wall for everyone to see."

A friend beamed at me as I was walking back to my room that evening.

"Hello, Maya," she said grasping my hand.

"Hello, Carrie," I said looking into her eyes. She looked tired and had dark lines under her eyes.

"You look very tired," I ventured to remark.

"I slept only for two hours last night," Carrie said.

She was the girl from Germany I had met at the party soon after I had come, and I remembered what she had told me about herself "I have to seek my fortune here," she had said. Born of poor parents, she had to make her way alone ever since she was twelve years old. It was the bright tingle of money that always urged her to move on and grab at the opportunity to come to America. She was willing to work day and night and go to any lengths to meet important people. She did not worry about what people thought if she could persuade, manipulate and get people to do whatever she wanted. I knew that she was far cleverer than she pretended to be.

"This country is terrible," she had once whispered to me, "It is run by women. Did you see those boys there? They are mere dough in the hands of girls. We can manipulate them anyway we want... the poor devils ... they always think of only one brief passage to the dream world."

"Won't you like to marry one of them yourself?" I had asked her playfully.

"Oh! I don't want one of those poor fools. One can never be sure of them. They vacillate like butterflies among flowers. I want to marry an elderly man - well-settled, mature and with lots of money."

"He better be one who knows that it is difficult to get a young wife," I said to myself and silently acknowledged her scheming brains.

"Shall we go and eat somewhere?" asked Carrie. She was evidently looking for company; she had said that she did not feel good about eating alone. An informal friendship had existed between me and her from the first day we met. There was something pathetically unavoidable in everything she did and she must have found the need to talk to someone who didn't have to be included in her future plans. I was casual and remote enough to give a patient hearing to her random thoughts. The cafeteria was not far, we spoke of work and people as we walked towards it. She had some shrewd remarks to pass on people in general.

"They seem to be always figuring out what you will ask them," she said, "they have a questioning glance as though asking you, 'what do you want?' They are sure that everyone has some ulterior motive. There is so much distrust here especially against foreigners. But don't you know that they all came to this country only like us? They might have come earlier, but their motives were the same as ours. No good human relations here - they are all alienated from the others."

It surprised me to hear such ideas on America coming from a newcomer. Carrie was proving to be too mature for her years. She seemed to have no illusions on life (like poor me!); she had set herself to live deliberately on cold calculation. All she could do in a hostile world was to fight it in its own terms. I could not but rue my own feeble attempts to stand up against the hostile world when I compared myself to her. I had for all these years lived only with vague ideals and emotional responses, and was now being faced with reality in the New World, its terror and its fascination.

There was a long line at the cafeteria and we took our place in the queue for a long time. There were so many delicious items on the menu which cast their inviting splendour, but I had lost my appetite in my ruminations. I quietly took a plate of salad and fruits while Carrie joined me with a big pot of chocolate cream pie and a mounting height of double hamburgers. She chattered on as she fell greedily on her victuals. She might look for the job of a theatre attendant in the summer and she could then do something else during the day. It *might* also bring her face-to-face with an old millionaire strolling lazily to watch a play in the hope of recharging his romantic dreams. She might even find someone to massage during the day on handsome wages. It was certainly better than the secretarial work she was now constrained to do. Her words floated in the air and blended with reality. I looked at a lonely young man sitting in a corner opposite and smoking a chain of cigarettes. His unruly hair hung forward on his forehead and he did not care even to push them back to their place. He sat with a dreamy look watching the curling smoke with an empty plate in front of him. "What are you going to do in summer?" Carrie asked me loud enough to be heard. "I don't know," I replied feebly.

XIV

A students' seminar on Walt Whitman had been arranged by the Department and I could attend as an onlooker. I entered a room in which scholars sat around a long table and gestured to each other as they put across their points. It was as if the great body of Whitman's works was now within the total grip of these eager scholars who were determined to squeeze the last drops of his meanings ... they wanted to bring an ultra modem approach to Whitman ... they would read his subtext for subtle hidden meanings. One of the scholars was quoting from the text:

> I have said that the soul is not more than the body
> And I have said that the body is not more than the soul
> A scent of this armpit's aroma finer than prayer
> I merely stir, press, feel with my fingers and am happy
> To touch my person to someone else's is about as much as
> I can stand.

"Whitman's universal love is nothing but a kind of homosexuality in which he indulged whenever he could," he concluded. "His body was the reality ... His soul was his boast," said another with a twinkle in his eye. Another raised his hand and stood up to emphasise his point of view, "No, no, it's not homosexuality ... How could we then account for the more than psychologically normal sense of attachment he had for animals? Take this for example:

> Do not call the tortoise unworthy
> because she's something else
> The look of the bay mare shames
> Silliness out of me ...

Don't you see an abnormal passion here for all creatures including animals? If it is not sexual passion, what is it?" For a moment there was no answer from the crowded room. Soon started a murmur of voices and someone banged on the table for silence. Then a voice loud and clear announced, "it's coffee break now. Let us give it a thought and reassemble."

I do feel exasperated with all this hair splitting and digging for subtexts. More than anything else it is the sexual innuendo attached to all the sensitive lines and meanings in these literary texts that bothers and disturbs me. After those early days in my childhood when sex and its baton-wielding authority and harassment had threatened to erase my humanity and the rosy dreams of my aspirations, and had mingled poison with the very fibre of my flesh and blood, I had shunned and revolted against the intrusions of sexual implications in idealistic expressions. Do you call it puritanical or do you say it is a real felt antipathy of the spirit to the sordidness of flesh? When I read poems I get carried away by the ring and movement of words... their pitch and evocative quality ... the truth of their claims and splendid associations ... but here in America to be an academic is to analyse, rip apart and generate sexual explanations. I must confess that I am unfit for such operations ... am I being forced here to change, to remake myself? Or else will those Bs and Cs haunt me throughout and turn me into what they label as a 'drop-out'? Now as I move out towards the 'Exit' from the Whitman seminar I see and hear the scholars reassemble and plead vigorously to throw out old ideas in order to make room for new terms and labels. I try to remember who had labelled the Americans as forming a lonely crowd. Aren't these American authors and critics totally alienated from normal ways of seeing things? Each of them has his/her own individual obsession to pursue, but they can gain success /sale of their ideas only by putting them up as interesting to the community.

I have seen many young writers and artists gather together to revile the establishment, Vietnam war, parental pressures and materialistic pursuits. The young males among them often had long beards, dreamy eyes and a relaxed air... the bushy growth around their mouths glistened with drops of coca cola they sipped every now and then, and the girls were wrapped in exotic costumes that looked like blankets with unusual designs and prints of birds and animals. All of them were particularly kind to foreigners who stared at them with a mixture of envy and astonishment. Their only pursuit seems to be their own special identity which they would make the world acknowledge ... no illusions of material success, achievements, sacrifice or compromise ever claimed their attention, these boys and girls were wrapped up only in protest and passive performance. Facts and fiction, truth and illusions, being and seeming, intermingle promiscuously perhaps in my awareness as I keep watching them and I feel more troubled than I ever was back home where it was only the sorry parade of people caught in a network of their daily pursuits of food, work, medicines for themselves and their families that used to fill me with a sense of desperation leading nowhere... Will the world end with a bang or just a whimper?

As I came out of the seminar room I had to walk across the familiar corridor ... Professor Healy sat on his seat, cool and firm, filling out entries on individual report cards of students. With an overwhelming urgency to communicate whatever was seething within me I started telling him how frustrated I was...

"I didn't want to do this kind of research," I said, "I thought that the America I would see would be the America described by Whitman in his Preface. But what do I see here! There seems to be nothing that is sacred or inviolate here. I feel like pulling my hair and shrieking ... this kind of education will lead to violence. I just can't...",

Loud peals of laughter coming from the stooping old man stopped me mid-way in my effusions. "I am only a PhD.," he said as he continued to laugh, "I am not an M.D.... a poor and weak creature that I am, I cannot claim to understand women, ha! ha! ha!"

I felt the edge of bitterness and fun in his voice, but there was insult too, a slap on my face... the nervous rhythms of my speech came to a sudden halt, my muted voice hovered only as the falling echoes of a strong note struck on the stretched strings of a violin ... strings that well-nigh broke with sudden pressure and now gasped to regain a semblance of stability ... one could see them writhing in continuous vibrations... the released echoes floated around with dark halting motion. He looked steadily at my confusion as I turned around and dragged my weary steps towards my room.

MELTING POT

I

That was indeed a wake-up call for me ... that encounter with the old man and his unconcealed amusement at my plight. I had rushed to him to confide my innermost trepidations and share my fears, but he had tried to label me as a psychotic! "I am only a PhD," he had said, "I am not an M.D". Does it mean that I have to go to a doctor or psychiatrist rather than to a teacher or a class? My sense of maladjustment and disorientation, my desperation in the midst of the cultural divide that forced me to look at everything around me differently from everyone else had brought me to this condition. Professor Healy' s harsh analysis and pronouncement on my abnormal mental make-up stung me deeply and challenged my fighting spirits. We, Indians, belong to an ancient culture that had developed a sense of veneration and mystic awe towards language, art and other natural phenomena, but the Americans of recent origins in history had distinguished themselves in a process of ruthless analysis and getting to the bottom of the material context of everything ... they did not hesitate to let man be reduced to a bare, forked animal with an erect penis between the legs that always urged him to go on and on...

Clinging to the past as I did was probably the root of my problem... looking at the present with eyes smeared with the past had become an addiction to me, comparing all that was happening with whatever happened in the past was getting me nowhere in America where I wanted to start a new life**. "Down with history!" I heard myself saying, "Down with all prejudices and old ways!"** One has to go on living in an ascending scale with no backward look or scruple... No chewing the cud of bygone days.. That seemed to be the answer I was searching for, that was the American answer.

I now started dreaming of the changes I would freely allow to overtake me. I shall break out from the chains of the past that hold me to comparison and rumination and I will go all out for whatever came my way.

A sequence of shrill sounds from the phone got me jumping up from my seat.

"Maya, I am Hamid ... do you remember meeting me at the party?"

"Which party? When?"

"Last Saturday, you know... our hostess, Mrs McMohan, introduced us and said that we should make friends. I am Hamid from Pakistan."

Oh! That boy... my memory gurgled up at once and tried to warn me ... Mrs McMohan had brought him to me and said, "here is Hamid ... he is alone here having left his wife behind in Pakistan. Since you are also alone here, it might be a good idea for you to meet and get together."

"Wouldn't they make a fine pair ..." I had heard someone whispering near me with a raucous giggle and then I had moved away.

So, now Hamid was calling me. Should I shun his offer or go along with him? *(no prejudices, please ... my new inner voice was mumbling... Down with History!)*

"Yes, Hamid ... I remember."

"Would you like to go with me to a poetry reading session? I have taken a course in American poetry and we are having an evening of poetry. A very smart Professor in campus is reading his latest poems. Would you come?"

"Where shall I meet you?"

"I shall come to your hostel and pick you up."

So that was how it all began. A short and rather darkish Pakistani with eager bulging eyes came to pick me up and I was ready to go with him. The daughter of an orthodox Brahmin family all geared up to forget her past inhibitions and memories and opening up to accept new experiences... ***(it means nothing... an inner voice told me, one can do whatever one likes in America ... no one is watching you ...)***

The poems being read were atrocious according to my taste, but I decided to listen and locate their unique quality. I heard the word 'copulation' being repeated every now and then and used to rhyme with 'exaltation', 'liberation', 'masturbation', 'meditation' and so on. The reader often paused at these words with a sense of hidden meanings, but no such meanings were stated or spelt out. The audience hung on those words with silent suspense before breaking out into a twitter. Was it only a technique of entertainment played at high pitch, I wondered, since no one seemed to bother about any message. It was only a performance, a host of contrasts and similarities released from their social contexts ... I could see Hamid shaking with enjoyment engaged in virtual fantasies.

"What a super performance," everyone murmured when the show came to an end.

II

"I want to sign up for his class in Poetry," I told Hamid. He, what's his name, seems to generate so much fun by disassociating meanings from sounds. One needs no longer to be tied to deeper meanings which inhibit our freedom. I would like to understand how he teaches that."

Hamid tried to squeeze my hands as I said this. "You know so much, Maya. Can I see you again?"

I was a late entrant in Professor Ainsworth's class. Will he teach anything about poetry, or will he only put up a performance, I wondered. Doesn't a coin have two different sides?

He was in the midst of talking about Aristotle and Plato. Aristotle had started it all... he said, our minute preoccupation with individuals and details... Plato kept himself to abstractions ... he had no use for poets who dwelt on individuals and their sensibilities. But Aristotle, a student of Plato, had toppled his teacher upside down and led to the developments in the western world today. Aristotle's preoccupation with Nature showed the way to Nomenclature and an analysis of all objects, the exploration and exploitation of nature and finally to the great laceration that dwells in the heart of everyone. If we had left it all to Plato we would still have been playing with abstractions and kept ourselves happily immune... as some cultures still did in the East.

I somehow got an impression that he was talking to me and making a reference to Indian philosophy. So I stood up and asked him:

"Don't we all still have some abstract rules to go by? Are not our societies still based on some abstract rules that bind all individuals?"

"No, no, my dear," he turned his glaring eyes on me who had inadvertently asked the question. "Not in America ... no such society in America ... only individuals and their whims.. Is it not different from where you come?"

I was silenced. Those abstract rules in my countrythat ignored individuals, their needs and differences had laid their iron hands on me and made me rebellious to break out from their clutches. It was my sense of my own difference that had driven me to seek shelter in America and brought me to a sad and confused state. I had protested against the norms and rules of my society and tried to find my path in a different direction and I had not yet found my answers.

My eyes were glistening with tears as I left the class and went to my room. I then sat in front of a blank sheet of paper and started scribbling my reactions to what I had heard. Wiggly black scrawls covered the blank page as I experienced an onrush of powerful feelings.

> Speak not to me of Duty
> Duty that waits on Absurdity
> Rats in narrow alleys
> Mistake the burning lights
> Of cat's eyes
> As leading lights

"·Would you call this poetry?' I wrote at the end of my almost automatic scribbling and waited next day at the door of Professor Ainsworth for his comments on my first-ever attempt at writing poetry. It was his reading of poetry and his class that had inspired me thus and I almost hung on his lips for his comments. But he didn't seem to be impressed by my efforts and mumbled that it was full of those abstractions he wanted to avoid.

"You need imagery in a poem to create a sense of immediacy," he said.

"What about those rats and cat's eyes in the poem? Are they not images?"

"But you should never make a statement in a poem. The imagery should be allowed to generate an immediate emotional complex."

"What do you mean?" I said, "The emotions are within the person who experienced them and so naturally there will be a statement from that person."

"Ha! Ha!" he laughed aloud his eyes gleaming and showing a beautiful set of teeth. "You are quite off the track, madam, if you think that a poem is for the expression of personal feelings. Haven't you read Eliot's Tradition and Individual Talent? A poem is not for self-expression and it leads to an extinction of personality. It is achieved through the use of imagery that create an immediate emotional complex. Have you read Ezra Pound's imagist poem,

In a station of the Metro? Go and read it. It was that poem that led to the great Imagist movement in Modem Poetry."

This was indeed more than I could hope to chew. But I was determined to understand. If this totally new approach to one's experiences and their transformation into imagery could offer me at least a brief respite from my compulsive obsession with my past and lure me away from indulging in general statements and abstractions I might as well work at it with Professor Ainsworth's help. It could lead me to start a new chapter in my life in America.

Henceforth Professor Ainsworth and poetry became my new obsession. I thought nothing of rushing to his room almost every day with some new questions on poetry and scraps of my own poems. "Is this poetry?" I often asked him, "Does this manage to bring an air of impersonality and do away with personal emotions?" Serious questions these, but they often sounded rather churlish when I hurled them at him in my efforts to become an American poet.

Truth tucked into beauty
Is poetry ... (Iwrote)
Poetry is droppings from the mind
A mind that wrestles all alone
With broken phrases in a broken world.
It comes as whirlwind from the depths
Breaks the bonds and roams astray
Crumbling idols brought to port
Droppings from Eternity.
Do not think of poetry with desire
Fly into her arms
Like pollens strewn by air
It comes on the verge of tearing up a dream
And it is composed of dreams, tears and anger.

"You persist with your moral air," he said, "but I do notice some sexual imagery in your work." He had a glitter in his impish eyes as he said it and I was charmed by his good humour.

"But how about some fine use of rhyme and alliteration? Poetry is made up of sounds only and it is the fine organisation and manipulation of sounds that make an effective poem ... Technique! Technique! Technique and performance are all that matter. Think of music ... does it ever make a statement?" He concluded and moved away.

I was convinced that a whole new world was opening out for me. One no longer needed to brood on the real happenings in one's life and the limitations imposed by the rigid sequence and the flow of feelings generated by them. One needs to have only a sharp eye on effects to be produced on others. One needs to manipulate the experiences and present them in bits and pieces as effective images and sounds to be used in performance for others... how else could one be rid of the personal burden? Is that what art means in America? Is art here trying to displace life?

III

In the meantime my classes with other teachers went on as usual. I tried to corroborate whatever I was learning from Ainsworth with what these other teachers put forward as their views on art and literature.

One day Professor Beardsley was going on analysing the novels of 19th century women writers. He seemed to be quite fascinated with Kate Chopin's novel, *The Awakening*. The title immediately produced all round reverberations of curiosity and interest. Even the backbenchers with bored and sleepy eyes sat up to listen to his explication. Awakening to what? Spiritual, physical or simply to a realm of fantasies that led her to another world after death?

"She seldom understood what she was going through," the Professor said, "She lived as a puppet set up and tuned by others according to social codes until she met this young man. Although she had a husband and a social position, her real self was not awakened and she had to go through a process of awakening. It was the fate of women in those days. Women were suppressed by men and their social codes that seldom gave a chance to women to come to their own."

"Is a failed romance a way to liberation and awakening? Is it not just another set of illusions that finally leads to suicide?"

"One has to watch for the imagery in the text," Beardsley asserted. "The imagery will tell you what this awakening is all about. It was just a case of sexual awakening. Follow the chain of images from the beginning of the text... see how her sexual desire controlled by others gradually opens out for herself."

"But she was already married and had a child... was it not just an infatuation rather than an awakening?"

"Follow the sexual imagery ... her romance comes to its own in her need for sex other than what is controlled by others. ***That is the beginning of women's liberation.*** This book is the beginning of the Women's Liberation movement."

He then started opening out the text to read long passages from those pages which he had already marked profusely with yellow markers.

All this talk about the chain of sex imagery made me sit up and listen with rapt attention.

So it all came down to sex and sexual imagery to make a dent in one's consciousness. All those struggles for liberation and freedom from social restraints were nothing but battles for sexual freedom. Social factors did not count, it seems, when individuals had an opportunity to break through them. That class left me strangely excited and curious.

IV

Hamid called me again that evening. He asked me whether I had ever been to a night bar in the town outside the campus. When I said 'no', he urged me to accompany him.

"Maya, perhaps you have been brought up strictly by orthodox parents, but you have to shed those scales and give in to your own needs when you come to America. Come with me and have a taste of what real America is," he said.

I would have really liked to tell him what my life at home was really like and how I had yearned to escape from its clutches. But I kept quiet and merely said, "Oh! Why not? You will bring me back here, won't you?"

"Of course!"

I had never so far accompanied a young man to taste nightlife outside the campus. I remembered the scenes from my last New Year party and anticipated meeting people drinking and dancing merrily. I wondered whether I should agree to dance with Hamid if he asked me. But I was immediately stung with the thought that I had no idea how to dance. Will I not make a fool of myself?

Almost everyone stared at us as we entered. I felt I could read their thoughts. They might have recognised us as a Pakistani and an Indian ... students wishing to escape to an anonymous place for a little romance. The shows were on and there were no bolts barred in people's behaviour. Couples stood here and there engaged in long kissing sessions and some others were just sitting glued to their drinks as they watched the others and talked at random.

Hamid brought me a drink and put his hand on mine, "Have you ever been kissed, Maya?" he asked me.

I started feeling nervous all on sudden. I knew that I was not up to accepting a kiss from Hamid. I rued myself for coming so far and being so vulnerable.

"No, no, Hamid, I would not like that... Let us go home after this drink."

But someone from the back had already recognised Hamid. He came up rather aggressively and asked, "What are you doing here with that girl? Are you blackies trying to ape the west?"

Suddenly almost everyone had gathered around us. Some one took me by my arms and tried to dance... Hamid tried to snatch me from him and knocked him down. Confusion, chaos, broken glasses, abuses and blows. I stood there among them being pulled in different directions and suddenly I was trying to extricate myself and managed to take to my heels. As I came out to the parking lot I could not even find Hamid's car. I trembled at the thought of being pursued by all of them and finally it was Hamid who came out with several cuts on his face, crestfallen and agitated and drove me home.

Back in my room I sat alone for a long time in front of a blank paper and waited for words to ooze out of my cramped mind.

I was meeting Professor Ainsworth again and again in his room although I had finished his course on poetry with a modest B+ grade. I was not ready to give up my search for answers to questions on art and poetry which I felt sure he kept somewhere up his sleeve. Some of his statements and answers were drawing me closer to him and I loved the way he could release me from nagging doubts and fears. Do those images and techniques used in his poems originate from the heart or the nerves, I wanted to ask him. Or was it the solar plexus that was involved? But I did not dare to pose such foolish questions.

One day he drew my attention to the poems of Wallace Stevens and spoke to me about the poem titled *Thirteen Ways of Looking at a Blackbird.* "Go and read that," he said, "it will tell you how not to look at things from a single point of view. In fact there are as many ways as there are people and seconds and one can have as many perspectives. Poetry is all about grasping those differences and translating them into words." I welcomed his words and the flexibility in viewpoints that it brought to my cramped mind - it was like treating a wound with fresh air and I clung to his wisdom. I felt I was starting to grow like a sapling freshly aired and nourished and a rare sense of exhilaration overwhelmed my senses. "One can always be different from all the others. Nature has provided for all sorts of differences. One need not feel inferior or ashamed for that." I said to myself.

"Americans believe that everything is possible," he said one day. "it is all a question of rewiring that part in your cerebral cortex called the Amygdala. If you are wired into one way of thinking you have to unstitch those steel threads to feel differently."

"All experiences are experimental in nature," he pointed out once. "There is only flux in nature, and no permanent stability. Imitate nature and survive."

Soon his lithe, attractive figure and animated expressions came to be installed in the portals of my mind as one of those enigmatic God figures that I had seen in temples in my childhood to which people paid obeisance without knowing their actual powers.

THE HORROR!

I

The campus life around me was changing drastically during those days. The students, women, young people as well as the minorities and several such social groups were corning to their own and asserting their rights against the authority of the establishment. Books such as *The Organization Man, Hidden Persuaders* and *Catcher in the Rye* became favourite points of discussion and debate and Holden Caulfield was projected as a hero victimised by society. Long processions and marches against the Vietnam War, shooting of student protesters by National Guards and sit-ins led by drop-outs and Hippies became common sights in the campus and it seemed as though the world was turning topsy-turvy in America. And then the mothers and daughters - the women of America were reading Virginia Woolf and Betty Friedan to escape the constraints of that mystic enclosed space built around their home and hearth.

I got invited to a Women's Liberation meeting. The women I saw there, most of them scantily clad, bra-less, rebellious and intensely articulate, were readily slipping into tears and red eyes while giving graphic account of some form of harassment endured and enduring under the male chauvinistic regime. It really made me gasp on hearing the different kind of cruelties that existed in America which women as a subclass had to put up with.

"You... the girl from India come to the forefront ..." someone called out for me, "We know what a raw deal is meted out to the women there even when they manage to escape all those attempted murders within the womb and the cradle. Share your experiences with us..."

I knew that was my chance to share my private woes with the public. I wished to shout from rooftops whatever happened to me in my own house when I refused to accept a conventional marriage. However, as I tried to bleed out my past wounds, words failed and I was nearly choked. "Buck up, girl, next time. We know how you feel." Someone said before calling the next speaker.

Do they really know, I wondered. Can I ever manage to tell them about all those voiceless, suppressed agonies endured not only by me, but all the others... widows like Amrnalu, girls like Mala, and wives like my own mother***? Is there a common ground on which I could be sure when I speak to these women***?

"My husband," I overheard someone saying as we were leaving the meeting which finally ended as a wishy-washy affair with everyone weeping and holding each other,

"I think he is dead. He went away to Mexico or Africa and was murdered in a riot."

Those were by no means the best of times to live in an American campus. The pressures of the Vietnam War were telling on the American students, while the foreign students enjoyed immunity from mandatory military draft. The foreigners were very hesitant to speak on the situation and comment on the policies of the establishment and this set them apart as an alien presence against the turbulent background. No point in siding with the American students while one remained immune to their woes and no way to criticise an authority that wielded power over one's very presence within the charmed circle. One had to learn to be non committal and defer all opinions to cultivate the art of silence and cunning in the land of the exile. Besides, authority in America was never blatantly visible or gruesome to those who were used to more severe forms of its self-righteous presence in their own countries.

An explosive topic that often came up in theme writing and discussion those days was the Vietnam War and its consequences on the nation. Federal laws were found to be in conflict with individual needs and conscience - and dissensions and disputes became very common. An exemption from draft was what every freshman wished for and they were prepared to go to any lengths to get away. I wondered what the American professors had to say to the students to comfort them in their plight. They could well advise them to get those high grades in class which brought them exemption from military recruitment, but the basic conflict between the rules of the establishment and individual needs remained unresolved. When I witnessed so much discontent, arguments and confusions prevailing among students, I wondered how anyone could try to translate such strong feelings into an impersonal cluster of imagery in a poem. How could anyone think of writing poetry at all in the thick of such burning issues? My own efforts in this direction filled up a page, however, and I found that I had written the following lines almost all of them as blatant statements!

Sublimation of an exasperation
Is what I would call confusion.
Confusion without organisation
Is what I think would cause a mutation.
Ideas like fads crackled into sparks,
Verbs venomous like worms wriggled into shapes,
Sentences -those gently heaving things
Shrank into themselves at the very touch,
An answer that erupts sheds itself like leaves
The facial muscles tense yawned themselves asleep.

II

I could hear loud voices all around me as I sat in my corner of the large hall with a bunch of student papers in front of me. It was all quiet when I had walked up to my seat, but suddenly there were these loud voices, arguments and abuses rising to an incredible pitch.

At the other end of the hall where Miss Cameroon used to sit, students had gathered and were arguing with her. A teacher in an American university wields the sole power of giving grades to those registered for his/her course and it is considered foolish to have an argument with teachers who can ruin your records and your career prospects with a red mark from their pens. Better to drop out or slip away from a course if one cannot get on with a teacher. But now these arguments and abusive words rattled me and all the others around. "You get out... out from here," Miss Cameroon was shouting. "You old witch... don't try to force your sop on us," came the reply. "Call the campus police," someone shouted and then they all marched out. They were a group of bedraggled youth with pinched faces in ill-fitting clothes.

This was most unusual. Discontents and conflicts were generally pressed down and smoothed over with mellifluous words and now they were being suddenly let off openly. Cameroon stood up and shouted, "Those bastards! They tried to humiliate me in the class, not only me, but our whole nation. They should go and speak on the streets and not in my class."

Dissent is widely accepted in America, even in classrooms. One could say whatever one wanted to, but no one needs to listen or disagree. Violent situations are avoided this way and personal equations do not matter. Obviously in this case, tensions were blown over rather aggressively, but none of the listeners wanted to know more. Of course the system could take care of itself... the disciplinary committee and ombudsman would look into the matter.

Skirting around a violent situation seemed more effective than confronting it and trying to root it out, it seems. The universities provided academic space for keeping conflicts and violence at bay and once this space was intruded upon, unthinkable chaos might be the consequence. Can the impersonal space occupied by art and discursive space provided by universities stem the tide of inner chaos and violence?

Next day I heard bits and snatches of disturbing news as I came to my desk. Cameroon's house had burnt down during the night, they said, and she had barely escaped with severe burns. They were going round taking a collection for her since she had lost everything, her clothes, books and all. "Where is she?" I asked excitedly... "who set fire to her house?" Some of them stared at me on this and one replied quite coolly, "We did not hear that it was set fire to... it might have been just an electrical failure... The house was built with wood and an electrical fire could destroy it."

"We have to help her," someone said. "She has insurance all right... She can move into another place soon enough."

No talk of arson, no backbiting on yesterday's events, no blames, no needles of suspicion, no attempts to establish connections ... the fire had just happened as an act of nature ... one has to do all one can to help the victim. I had to bite my tongue to stop myself saying anything about the possible student outrage against her.

At last I seem to have got into the secret of what makes America great. ***America lives on by its image, by what is said about it and not by what is hidden and unspoken. It is the image rather than reality that matters most in America and the American Experiment remains the greatest human effort to liberate humanity from the intrusions of the truth of human condition. Will the rest of the world understand this truth about America and Americans? How long does it take for one from another part of the world to slouch towards American dreams and reality?***

III

Then it was the outbreak of the Bangladesh War that threw fresh grit into my eyes that were beginning to see the American reality. To live in the campus during those days and not be drawn into controversial views and painful postures was nearly impossible. Almost all the Americans considered the war as an Indian act of aggression and it offended one's national pride and patriotism to agree with them or even to keep quiet. Words came steaming out of my pen to defend India and its humanitarian effort to help East Pakistanis against their military rulers. When one of my letters to the editor of a local paper decrying American insensibility got published I knew I was no longer welcome to stay on in America. India was being arraigned for its doublespeak ... its pretence of morality and non-violence and its blatant aggression against a sovereign nation.

Those professed claims for impersonality and escape from personal emotions deftly created a complex of words and images, and no longer appealed to the clamour going on within me. Should I not go back home and realign myself with my own people?

Then I got a letter from Ramunna recounting all the turmoil going on in the family and the country. That old patriarch, our father, has had a stroke and was lying unconscious for days in a coma. My mother distraught and helpless was reduced to a shadow... her mind shrinking away from the present. She seemed to find some sort of refuge only in blabbering about those days in the past when she had come to the family as a young bride. She wept endlessly looking at her husband who lay motionless with a blank look. Most of our old servants were dead or too old and there were not many around to do any work. Ammalu was dead a year ago after being laid up with swollen feet and acute body pain for several months. The feudal network of support for an old landed family had crumbled with toiling tenants asserting their claims on the land. Ramunna who had managed to hold on to a government job was trying his best to keep the family together. My sisters had somehow gone ahead with their studies and were looking for jobs in local schools. The stigma of having me as an older sister had affected their marriage prospects and the drop in the family fortunes had made them less attractive to eligible grooms. Both Hari and Balu were studying to be engineers and were living in cities.

Almost as if I wanted to search for a part of my seared flesh left behind at home, I decided to hurry back without a thought of what I would do after reaching there. As my friends and colleagues came to know of my impending departure, they were most kind and I was invited to a few farewell parties. Almost everyone was curious to know what I planned to do after my return and I spoke to them of social work and teaching as my probable fields of activity. I regretted my lack of training in these areas... if only I had managed to be a doctor as I had wanted to, would I not have a ready field to work?

Only two days were now left before my departure. I was all set with most of my baggage packed and all the farewells said when I heard the news. It was Hamid of all people who rang me up and told me that Professor Ainsworth was dead ... brutally murdered and left in his flat by unknown assailants. Students of all types from various countries and cultures used to visit him for prolonged poetry reading and discussions... he had several admirers as well as detractors... who knows what could have happened?

I felt as if I had been dealt a severe blow. All that I had tried to learn in America ... all those ideas of art and life, performance and personality, image and reality lay now in a heap of ruins. No way one can hope for an extinction of personality except in death and total oblivion.

I attended his funeral a day before I left. It was held in the Baptist church although the Professor was not known as a believer or churchgoer during his lifetime and had never bothered to mention church or God in his teaching. According to him the world was made up of pure sounds and sensations... he had always tried to catch and assemble them in order to present them to his audience in various combinations and transmutations. Students had flocked to him as though he was a new prophet doling out easy salvation, but now who among them had done this dire deed and silenced for ever his smart audition of sounds and sensations?

I looked at his body laid out and presented to appear whole and unscathed in clever funeral dressing ... all the wounds and scars carefully sewed up and covered, his mischievous gleaming eyes smoothly shut and that tuft of black hair falling over his forehead partially skewing his vision carefully combed down. I deeply mourned for all the hopes and illusions I had cherished about him and tears swelled in my eyes.

I had no time to keep my eyes and ears open for any rumours or follow up the results of the investigation into his murder. But in a very rare letter I received after I had reached home, it was mentioned that the culprit was suspected to be none other than a girl who used to frequent his home. He had many such liaisons, my informer noted, and he was very much what they called 'footloose and fancy free'. He always made up and bent his theories to suit his own convenience and pleasure and he did not have any emotion for anyone. He always used others to advance his own ideas and fancies.

As I crouched amidst my own luggage - several bags and suitcases brought from America, I wrestled with memories that overwhelmed me ... memories of the man who I had thought would help to save me from the undertow of my own emotions and vain efforts to slouch towards an American dream. ***Had I, I wondered, come across only a crouching terror and addressed it as my Saviour? Was he a man or monster? Am I a clown or a fool?***

RETURN HOME

"In my beginning is my end"

T.S. Eliot

RETURN HOME

All the windows were open as I walked into the large room where we, as children, used to spend the twilight hours. The huge branch of the tree that used to overshadow the roof wielding its power as a Sword of Damocles had at last been cut and sunlight poured into the room. My father lay mounted on a cot in a corner of the room and Ramunna looking grey and very thin stood by the cot.

"So, you have come back," he said. Like in those days when I used to come home quietly from the convent school, I had once again returned unannounced with my luggage.

"He is in a coma after the stroke. He does not show any recognition of anyone or anything. We are with him 24 hours of the day. There is no night or day for him or for us."

Yes, that is our life.. that is how we have to try to guard and keep watch over whatever is left of the past and of one's own family.

The few days I spent at home were haunted by memories.

But the worlds around me had managed to move very fast. This I had noticed even as I arrived at the airport with its large hall, a mounting number of trolleys, escalators and elaborate systems of security and control. A long line of cars, taxis, and buses whizzed past as I came out and for a moment I had a hazy feeling that I had not left America. Our old country was remaking itself along modern lines... when the old giant heaves itself out of its long slumber it will surely wear an American overcoat readily available now in all the sidewalk shops of the city.

I knew that I had now to fend for myself with no pressure, guidance or support from my family. I had to find myself a job to earn my living and make my own terms to live with the rest of the world.

As a last gesture for seeking some kind of support I still needed, I hastened to my old convent school to meet my old mentor. But I was told that Sister Sacramenta was no longer alive... she was peacefully dead in sleep and buried in the convent cemetery. All I could do now was to go to her grave and kneel there leaving all the rest to God just as she had instructed me.

I had made my life's journey so far as a pilgrimage seeking for freedom and guarding my right to be different from others. Now I knew the time had come for me to end my search and settle down with my understanding of Freedom in all its ramifications.

GLOSSARY

Akka:	A respectful term used to denote an elder sister
Amme!	Oh! Mother! -a desperate address to one's mother, or female deity
Annante cycline:	Means "for my brother's cycle"
Ararmperannol:	A child born on the sixth month. Usually the term is used to denote any one who is always in a hurry
Athai:	A respectful term for an elderly woman meaning 'aunt'
Bhadrakali:	The ferocious image of Lord Shiva's wife
Bhagavatar:	The musician who gives lessons in music
Bhagawat Gita:	Sacred Indian text that consists of Lord Krishna's lengthy discourses to Arjuna, his disciple, on human life and its various aspects and responsibilities
Chappals:	Open sandals
Chovan:	One of the scheduled castes
Devnagari:	A script in which Sanskrit and several dialects are written
Gayatri:	A very sacred mantra in Sanskrit to be chanted only by men
Ghee	Clarified butter
Gokul:	The place where Lord Krishna grew up as a young boy
Guagua:	Nonsense
Gud:	partly dried molasses
Hibiscus:	Red flowers liked by Gods and Goddesses who call for blood to shed to appease them
Hindi Pracharak:	'One who spreads the knowledge of Hindi
Illa:	Means "non-existent" or "not there"

Kajal:	A black dye used to mark the outline of eyes to enhance their beauty
Kali Yuga:	Evil end of a long cycle of Time that leads to Destruction
Karma:	Hindu Law of Retribution and Rewards for human beings for their actions through life
Kerosene lamp:	A lamp that burns on kerosene in places where there are no electric lights
Kolam:	designs made on the floor with rice powder
Krishna:	One of the incarnations of Vishnu (one of the Indian Trinities) who is depicted as young and jovial
Kumkum:	A reddish powder applied on the forehead to convey a sense of well being
Ladus:	A round sweet made with sugar, clarified butter and Lentil powder
Lungi:	A small strip of light cloth worn around the waist
Mahabhadrakali:	The ferocious consort of Lord Shiva. Prefix "maha" Is added to her name to denote her great power
Malayalam:	One of the Dravidian languages used as local language in Kerala
Mama:	maternal uncle
Mangal sutra:	A gold chain that a bridegroom ties around his wife's neck as a sign of marriage vow. It has an icon of Lord Shiva attached to it
Manni:	means sister-in-law, but at times even sons call their mother as manni
Mayakutty:	"Kutty is a suffix attached to names to show special affection
Mundu:	A long piece of cloth with a border which women tie around their Waist
Nair:	A caste name in Kerala that is lower to Brahmin. Nair consider themselves to be the original inhabitants of Kerala unlike Brahmins who are outsiders
Nadaswaram:	A musical instrument that produces sounds similar to that of a serpent

Narayana!Narayana! A chanting of God's name
Pandal: A decorated enclosed space in which large functions like marriages are conducted
Papadams: A fried snack in circular shape generally eaten with meals
Pattar: A derogatory term for Brahmins used by lower castes
Pattardom: The rule of pattars/ Brahmins
Petromax lamp: A sophisticated version of a kerosene lamp that produces a bright light using an incandescent mantle
Puja: A worship session that includes chanting, lighting of lamps and Incense and floral offerings
Raga: Melody
Ramayana: Sacred Indian Epic that narrates the Life and Times of Rama, one of incarnations of Lord Vishnu
Rikshaw: A vehicle pulled manually to carry people from place to place
Rudraksha: A chain of beads specially made from wood used to chant the many names of God
Sambhar: A common item in South Indian lunch menu made with lentils and vegetables cooked in tamarind juice
Sami: Master
Samsar: the vast sea of Life
Sar: A respectful suffix attached to personal names of elderly males/teachers
Saree: A long decorative piece of cloth worn by Indian women
Sloka: A stanza or a few lines that hang together inside a poem
Tambalam: A large brass tray used for making floral offerings to God
Travancore State: Southern part of the present Kerala State ruled in British times by a Maharaja (King)
Vadhyar: A Brahmin priest
Valya Sami: 'Valya' means big and 'Valya Sami' means big or grand master

Printed in the United States
By Bookmasters